GETTING THROUGH

JOHN McGAHERN

Getting Through

HARPER & ROW, PUBLISHERS

NEW YORK

Cambridge
Hagerstown
Philadelphia
San Francisco

London
Mexico City
São Paulo
Sydney

1817

FIRST U.S. EDITION

Library of Congress Cataloging in Publication Data

McGahern, John, 1934–
  Getting through.
  CONTENTS: The beginning of an idea.—
A slip-up—All sorts of impossible things. [etc.]
  I. Title.
PZ4.M14346Ge 1980 [PR6063.A2176] 823'.914 79–3667
ISBN 0–06–013043–1

80 81 82 83 84 10 9 8 7 6 5 4 3 2 1

To
ROBERT WOOF

The greater part of the book was written while I was British Northern Arts Fellow in the Universities of Durham and Newcastle upon Tyne, to whom I want to express gratitude.

Acknowledgements are due to the editors of the following, where the work first appeared: BBC 3, *Encounter, London Magazine, The New Review, Strand, Vogue.* 'The Wine Breath,' 'Gold Watch' and 'Sierra Leone' were first published in *The New Yorker.*

Contents

The Beginning of an Idea

The word Oysters was chalked on the wagon that carried Chekhov's body to Moscow for burial. The coffin was carried in the oyster wagon because of the fierce heat of early July.

Those were the first sentences in Eva Lindberg's loose notes, written in a large childish hand, and she started reading them at the table again as she waited for Arvo Meri to come to the small flat. The same pair of sentences was repeated throughout the notes in a way which suggested that she leaned on them for inspiration. *The word Oysters was chalked on the wagon that carried Chekhov's body to Moscow for burial. The coffin was carried in the oyster wagon because of the fierce heat of early July.* There was also among the notes a description of Chekhov's story called 'Oysters'.

The father and son were on the streets of Moscow in that rainy autumn evening. They were both starving. The father had failed to find work after trudging about Moscow for five months, and he was trying to muster up enough courage to beg for food. He had drawn the tops of a pair of old boots round his calves so that people wouldn't notice that his feet were bare under the galoshes. Above father and son was a blue signboard with the word *Restaurant* and on a white placard on the wall was written the word *Oysters*. The boy had been alive for eight years and three months and had never come across the word oysters before.

'What does oysters mean, Father?'

The father had touched a passerby on the sleeve, but not being able to beg he was overcome with confusion and stammered, 'Sorry.' Then he swayed back against the wall. He did not hear the boy's voice.

9

'What does oysters mean, Father?' the child repeated.

'It's an animal . . . it lives in the sea,' the father managed.

The boy imagined something between a fish and a crab, delicious made into a hot fish soup, flavoured with pepper and laurel, or with crayfish sauce and served cold with horseradish. Brought from the market, quickly cleaned, quickly thrown into the pot, quick-quick-quick, everyone was starving. A smell of steaming fish and crayfish soup came from the kitchen. The boy started to work his jaws, oysters, blessed oysters, chewing and slugging them down. Overcome by this feeling of bliss he grabbed at his father's elbow to stop himself from falling, leaned against the wet summer overcoat. His father was shivering with the cold.

'Are oysters a Lenten food, Father?'

'They are eaten alive . . . they come in shells, like tortoises but . . . in two halves.'

'They sound horrible, Father,' the boy shivered.

A frog sat in a shell, staring out with great glittering eyes, its yellow throat moving—that was an oyster. It sat in a shell with claws, eyes that glittered like glass, slimy skin; the children hid under the table, while the cook lifted it by its claw, put it on a plate, and gave it to the grown-ups. It squealed and bit at their lips as they ate it alive—claws, eyes, teeth, skin and all. The boy's jaws still continued to move, up and down; the thing was disgusting but he managed to swallow it, swallowed another one, and then another, hurriedly, fearful of getting their taste. He ate everything in sight, his father's galoshes, the white placard, the table napkin, the plate. The eyes of the oysters glittered but he wanted to eat. Nothing but eating would drive this fever away.

'Oysters. Give me some oysters,' he cried, and stretched out his hands.

'Please help us, sir. I am ashamed to ask but I can't stand it any more,' he heard his father's voice.

'Oysters,' the boy cried.

10

'Do you mean to say you eat oysters? As small a fellow as you eats oysters?' he heard laughter close. A pair of enormous men in fur coats were standing over him. They were looking into his face and laughing. 'Are you sure it's oysters you want? This is too rich. Are you sure you know how to eat them?' Strong hands drew him into the lighted restaurant. He was sat at a table. A crowd gathered round. He ate something slimy, it tasted of sea water and mould. He kept his eyes shut. If he opened them he'd see the glittering eyes and claws and teeth. And then he ate something hard, for it crunched.

'Good lord. He's eating the bloody shells! Don't you know you can't eat the shells? Here, waiter!'

The next thing he remembered was lying in bed with a terrible thirst, he could not sleep with heartburn, and there was a strange taste in his parched mouth. His father was walking up and down the small room and waving his arms about.

'I must have caught cold. My head is splitting. Maybe it's because I've eaten nothing today. I am quite useless. Those men must have spent ten roubles on the oysters today and I stood there and did nothing. Why hadn't I the sense to go up to them and ask them, ask them to lend me something? They would have given me something.'

Towards evening the child fell asleep and dreamt of a frog sitting in a shell, moving its eyes. At noon he was woken by thirst and looked for his father. His father was still pacing up and down and waving his arms around.

The word Oysters was chalked on the wagon that carried Chekhov's body to Moscow for burial. The coffin was carried in the oyster wagon because of the fierce heat of early July, she found she had written it down once more. Chekhov was that boy outside the restaurant with his father in the autumn rain, was that starving boy crunching the oysters in the restaurant while they laughed, was the child in the bed woken by thirst at noon, watching the father pace up and down the small room and waving his arms around. She wanted to write an imaginary

11

life of Chekhov, from the day outside the restaurant to the day the body of the famous writer reached Moscow in the oyster wagon for burial. It would begin with oysters and end with oysters, some of the oysters, after the coffin had been taken away for burial, delivered to the same restaurant in which the child Chekhov had eaten shells. She wasn't yet sure whether she would write it as a novel or a play. The theatre was what she knew best but she was sure that it would probably never get written at all unless more order and calm entered her life than was in it now. She closed the folder very quietly on the notes and returned them to their drawer. Then she showered and changed into a blue woollen dress and continued to wait for Arvo Meri to come.

That morning Arvo's wife had rung her at the theatre, where she was directing the rehearsals of Ostrovsky's *The Dragon*. At the end of much abuse she shouted, 'You're nothing but a whore,' and then began to sob hysterically. Eva used the old defence of silence and put down the receiver, and told the doorman that no matter how urgent any call claimed to be she was not to be interrupted in rehearsal. She was having particular difficulty with one of the leads, an actress of some genius who needed directing with a hand of iron since her instinct was to filch more importance for her own part than had been allotted to it. She had seen her ruin several fine plays by acting everybody else off the stage and was determined that it wasn't going to happen in this production. Once she began to rehearse again she put the call out of her mind but was able to think of nothing else during the midday break, and rang Arvo at his office. He was a journalist, with political ambitions on the Left, who had almost got into parliament at the last election and was almost certain to get in at the next. When he apologized for the call and blamed it on his wife's drinking she lost her temper.

'That makes a pair of you then,' and went on to say that she wanted a life of her own, preferably with him, but if not—

without him. She had enough of to-ing and fro-ing, of what she called his Hamlet act. This time he would have to make up his mind, one way or the other. He countered by saying that it wasn't possible to discuss it over the phone and arranged to call at her flat at eight. As she waited for him in the blue woollen dress after showering, she determined to have that life of her own. The two sentences *The word Oysters was chalked on the wagon that carried Chekhov's body to Moscow for burial. The coffin was carried in the oyster wagon because of the fierce heat of early July* echoed like a revenant in her mind and would not stay still.

There was snow on Arvo Meri's coat and fur hat when he came and he carried a sheaf of yellow roses. Once she saw the flowers she knew nothing would change. She laid them across a sheepskin that covered a large trunk at the foot of the bed without removing their wrapping.

'Well?'

'I'm so sorry about this morning, Eva. . . .'

'That doesn't matter,' she stopped him, 'but I do want to know what you propose to do.'

'I don't know what to do,' he said guiltily. 'You know I can't get a divorce.'

'I don't care about a divorce.'

'But what else is there to do?'

'I can take a larger flat than this. We can start to live seriously together,' she said, and he put his head in his hands.

'Even though there's nothing left between us she still depends on the relationship. If I was to move out completely she'd just go to pieces.'

'That's not my problem.'

'Can't we wait a little longer?'

'More than two years seems long enough to me. You go to Moscow by going to Moscow. If you wait until all the conditions are right you can wait your whole life.'

'I've booked a table at the Mannerheim. Why don't we talk it out there?'

'Why not?' she shrugged with bright sarcasm, and lifted the yellow roses from the sheepskin. 'I ask you for a life and you offer me yellow roses and a dinner at the Mannerheim,' but he did not answer as he started to dial a taxi, and she let the roses drop idly down on the sheepskin and pulled on her fur coat and boots and sealskin cap.

Charcoal was blazing in two braziers on tall iron stems on either side of the entrance to the Mannerheim. They hadn't spoken during the taxi drive and she remarked as she got out, 'They must have some important personage tonight.' She felt a sinking as in an aeroplane take-off as the lift went up. A uniformed attendant took their furs and they had a drink in the bar across from the restaurant while they gave their order to the waiter. The restaurant was half empty: three older couples and a very large embassy party. They knew it was an embassy party because of a circle of toy flags that stood in the centre of the table. Through the uncurtained glass they could see out over the lights of the city to the darkness that covered the frozen harbour and sea. He had drunk a number of vodkas by the time the main course came, and she was too tense to eat as she nibbled at the shrimp in the avocado and sipped at the red wine.

'You don't mind me drinking? I have a need of vodka to-night.'

'Of course not . . . but it won't be any use.'

'Why?' he looked at her.

'When I got pregnant you took me to the Mannerheim and said, "I don't know what to do. It's not the right time yet. That is all I know," and drank vodka and were silent for hours, except every now and then you'd say, "All I'm certain of is that it's not the right time yet for us to have a child." I had some hard thinking to do when I left the Mannerheim that night. And when I arranged for and had the abortion without telling you, and rang you after coming out of the clinic, you said the whole week had been like walking round under a dark cloud, but that I had made you so happy now. I was so understanding. One day we'd have a child when everything was right. And you came that evening with yellow roses and took me to the Mannerheim and later we danced all night at that place on the shore.'

She spoke very slowly. He didn't want to listen, but he didn't know what to say to stop her, and he ordered more vodka.

'And now when we spend three days in a row together your wife rings up and calls me a whore. You bring me yellow roses and take me to the Mannerheim. The vodka won't do any good. . . .'

'But what are we to do?'

'I've given my answer. I'll take a larger flat. We'll live together as two people, from now on.'

'But can't we wait till after the elections?'

'No. It's always been "wait". And there will always be something to wait for. They say there's no good time to die either. That it's as difficult to leave at seventy as at twenty. So why not now?'

'But I love you, Eva.'

'If you loved me enough you'd come and live with me,' and he went silent. He had more vodka, and as they were leaving she noticed the attendant's look of disapproval as he swayed into the lift. The tall braziers had been taken in, and as they waited while the doorman hailed a taxi he asked, 'Can I come back with you tonight?' 'Why not. If you want,' she laughed in a voice that made him afraid. He was violently ill when he got to the flat and then fell at once into a drugged sleep sprawled across the bed. She looked at him a moment with what she knew was the dangerous egotism of the maternal instinct before she made up a bed on the carpet and switched off the lights. He woke early with a raging thirst and she got him a glass of water. 'Was I sick last night?' 'Yes, but don't worry, in the bathroom.' 'Why didn't you sleep in the bed?' 'I'd have to wake you, the way you were in bed.' 'I'm sorry.' 'It doesn't matter.' 'Why don't you come in now?' 'All right,' she rose from the blankets on the floor. The night conversation seemed to her like dialogue from a play that had run too long and the acting had gone stale. He drew her towards him in the bed, more, she knew, to try to escape through pleasure from the pain of the hangover than from desire. She grew impatient with his tired fumbling and pulled him on top of her, provoking him with her own body till he came. Afterwards they both slept. She shook her head later when he asked her, 'When will we meet?' 'It's no use.' 'But I love you.' She still shook her head. 'I'm fond of you but you can't offer me what I want.' As he moved to speak she stopped him, 'No. I can't wait. I have work I want to do.' 'Is it that damned Chekhov's body?' 'That's right.' 'It'll never come to anything.' he said in hatred. 'I don't care, but I intend to try.' 'You're nothing but a selfish bitch.' 'I am selfish and I want you to go now.'

That morning there were several calls for her during rehearsals but she had left strict instructions that she wasn't to be disturbed, and when she got home that evening she took the phone off the hook.

She was surprised during the following days how little she yearned for him, it was as if a weight had lifted; she felt an affection for him that she felt for that part of her life that she had passed with him, but she saw clearly that it was for her own life and not for his that she had yearning. She would go on alone, and when he demanded to see her she met him with a calm that was indifference which roused him to fury. She had not built a life with him, she had built nothing: but out of these sentences *The word Oysters was chalked on the wagon that carried Chekhov's body to Moscow for burial. The coffin was carried in the oyster wagon because of the fierce heat of early July* she would build, and for that she had to be alone. She would leave this city that had so much of her past life, the theatre where she had worked so long. She would leave them like a pair of galoshes in the porch, and go indoors. She rang rich friends: Was their offer of the house in Spain still open? It was. They only used it in July. They would be delighted to loan it to her. She could be their cuckoo there till then. She went and offered her resignation to the old manager.

'But you can't leave in the middle of a production.'

'I'm sorry. I didn't explain properly. Of course I'll see the production through, but I won't be renewing my contract when it expires at the end of the year.'

'Is it salary?' he sat down behind his big desk and motioned to her to sit.

'No. I am leaving the theatre. I want to try to write,' she blurted out to save explanation.

'It's even more precarious than the theatre, and now that you've made your way there why throw it over for something worse still?' he was old and kindly and wise, though he too must have had to be ruthless in his day.

'I must find out whether I can or not. I'll only find out by finding out. I'll come back if I fail.'

'You know, contrary to the prodigal son story, few professions welcome back its renegades?'

'I'll take that risk.'

'Well, I see you're determined,' he rose.

As soon as a production begins to take shape it devours everybody around it so that one has no need for company or friends or anything outside it, and in the evening one takes a limp life home with no other idea but to restore it so that it can be devoured anew the next day. As she went home on the tram two days before the dress rehearsal she hadn't enough strength to be angry when she saw her photo in the evening paper and read that she was leaving the theatre to write. She was leaving to *try* to write. She should have been more careful. Kind as he was she should have known that the old manager would use any publicity in any way to fill the theatre. *To write* was better copy than the truthful *try to write*. She wondered

17

tiredly if there was a photo of the coffin being lifted out of the oyster wagon or of the starving man in his summer coat in the rain outside the restaurant while the boy crunched on the oyster shells within; and whether it was due to the kindness usually reserved for the dear departed or just luck, no production of hers had ever opened before to such glowing notices. And she left on New Year's Eve for Spain, by boat and train, passing through Stockholm and Copenhagen, and stopping five days in Paris where she knew some people. She had with her the complete works of Chekhov, and the two sentences were more permanently engraved than ever in her mind: *The word Oysters was chalked on the wagon that carried Chekhov's body to Moscow for burial. The coffin was carried in the oyster wagon because of the fierce heat of early July.*

She stayed five days in the Hotel Celtique on the rue Odessa, and all her waking hours seemed taken up with meeting people she already knew. Most of them scraped a frugal living from translation or journalism or both and all of them wrote or wanted to be artists in one way or another. They lived in small rooms and went out to cheap restaurants and movie houses. She saw that many of them were homesick and longed for some way to go back without injuring their self-esteem, and that they thought her a fool for leaving. In their eyes she read contempt. 'So she too has got the bug. That's all we need. One more,' and she began to protect herself by denying that there was any foundation to the newspaper piece. On the evening before she took the train to Spain she had dinner in a Russian restaurant off the Boulevard St Michel with the cleverest of them all: the poet Severi. He had published three books of poems, and the previous year she had produced a play of his that had been taken off after a week though it was highly praised by the critics. His threadbare dark suit was spotless, and the cuffs and collar of the white shirt shone, the black bow knotted with a studied

18

carelessness. They were waited on by the owner, a little old hen of a Russian woman, who spoke heavily accented French, and whose thinning hair was dyed carrot. A once powerful man played an accordion at the door.

'Well, Eva Lindberg, can you explain to me what you're doing haring off to Spain instead of staying up there to empty that old theatre of yours with my next play?' the clever mordant eyes looked at her through unrimmed spectacles with ironic amusement.

'I was offered a loan of a house there,' she was careful.

'And they inform me you intend to write there. You know there's not room for the lot of us,' he did not let up.

'That's just a rumour that got into a newspaper.'

'What'll you do down there, a single woman among hordes of randy Spaniards?'

'For one thing I have a lot of reading to catch up on,' she was safe now, borrowing aggression from his aggression.

'And why did you leave the theatre?'

'I felt I was getting stale. I wasn't enjoying it any more.'

'And have you money?'

'I have enough money. And what about your work?'

He started to describe what he was working on with an even more ferocious mockery that he usually reserved for the work of others. The accordion player came round the tables with a saucer and bullied those who offered him less than a franc. They had a second carafe of red wine and finished with a peppered vodka. Warmed by the vodka he asked her to sleep with him, his face so contorted into a fury at having to leave himself open to rejection that she felt sorry for him.

'Why not?' he pushed, soon he would begin to mock his own desire.

'I've told you,' she said gently enough. 'I've had enough of sleeping, with the Arvo business. I want to be alone for a time.'

She was left completely alone for the whole of the journey the next evening and night, going early to her sleeper, changing at the frontier the next morning into the wider Spanish train, which got into Barcelona just before noon. A taximan took her to the small Hotel New York in the Gothic quarter and it proved as clean and cheap as he said it would be. She stayed five days in Barcelona and was happy. As an army in peacetime she was doing what she had to do by being idle and felt neither guilt nor need to strive to make the holiday, always the death of any chance of actually enjoying it.

She walked the narrow streets, went to a few museums and churches, bought a newspaper on the Ramblas, vivid with the flower stalls under the leafless trees in the cold dry weather, and ate each evening at the Casa Agut, a Catalan restaurant a few minutes walk from the hotel. She sat where she could watch the kitchen, and always had Gaspacho, ensalada and a small steak with a half-bottle of red Rioja, enjoying the march of the *jefe* who watched for the slightest carelessness, the red and white towel on his shoulder like an epaulet. After five such days she took the train to Valencia, where she got the express bus to Almería. She would get off at Vera and get a taxi to the empty house on the shore. It was on this bus that she made her first human contact since leaving Paris, a Swedish homosexual who must have identified her as Scandinavian by her clothes and blonde hair and who asked if he could sit beside her. 'How far are you going?' she asked when she saw she was stuck with him for the journey. 'I don't know. South. I can go as far as I want,' though the hair was dyed blond the lines in the brittle feminine face showed he was sixty or more. He spoke only his own language and some English, and was impressed by her facility for acquiring languages. She wondered if the homosexual love of foreignness was that having turned away from the mother or been turned away they needed to do likewise with their mother tongue. 'Aren't you a lucky girl to find languages so easy?' She resented the bitchiness that inferred a boast she hadn't made.

'It's no more than being able to run fast or jump. It means you can manage to say more inaccurately in several languages

20

what you can say better in your own. It's useful sometimes but it doesn't seem very much to me if that's all it achieves.'

'That's too deep for me,' he was resentful and impressed and a little scared. 'Are you on a holiday?'

'No. I'm going to live here for a time.'

'Do you have a house?'

'Yes. I've been loaned a house.'

'Will you be with people or alone?' his questioning grew more eager and rapid.

'I'll be alone.'

'Do you think I could take a room in the house?'

She was grateful to be able to rest her eyes on the blue sea in the distance. At least it would not grow old. Its tides would ebb and flow, it would still yield up its oyster shells long after all the living had become the dead.

'I'm sorry. One of the conditions of the loan is that I'm not allowed to have people to stay,' she lied.

'I could market for you and cook.'

'It's impossible. I'm sorry,' he would cling to any raft to shut out of mind the grave ahead.

'You? Are you going far?' she diverted.

'The bus goes to Almería.'

'And then?'

'I don't know. I thought to Morocco.'

She escaped from him in Alicante, where they had a half-hour break and changed buses. She saw the shirtsleeved porters pat the Swede's fur coat in amusement, '*Mucho frío, mucho frío,*' as they transferred it to the boot of the bus returning to Almería, and she waited till she saw him take the same seat in the new bus, and then took her place beside an old Spanish woman dressed in black who smelled of garlic and who, she learned later, had been seeing her daughter in hospital. She felt guilty at avoiding the Swede so pointedly but it would be worse to join him again now as it would be to get up and leave him if she were with him, as once alive it is better to go on than

21

die, the best not to have been born at all, and she did not look back when she got off at Vera.

The house was low and flatroofed and faced the sea. The mountain was behind, a mountain of the moon, sparsely sprinkled with the green of farms that grew lemon trees and had often vine or olive on terraces of stone built on the mountain side. In the dried-up beds of rivers the cacti flourished. The village was a mile away and had a covered market built of stone and roofed with tiles the colour of sand. She was alarmed when the old women hissed at her when she first entered the market but then she saw it was only their way of trying to draw people to their stalls. Though there was a fridge in the house she went every day to the market, and it became her daily outing. The house had four rooms but she arranged it so that she could live entirely in the main room.

She reread all of Chekhov, ate and drank carefully, and in the solitude of her days felt her life for the first time in years in order. And the morning came when she decided to face the solitary white page. She had an end, the coffin of the famous writer coming to Moscow for burial that hot July day; and a beginning, the boy crunching on the oyster shells in the restaurant while the man starved in his summer coat in the rain outside: what she had to do was to imagine the life in between. She wrote in a careful hand *The word Oysters was chalked on the wagon that carried Chekhov's body to Moscow for burial. The coffin was carried in the oyster wagon because of the fierce heat of early July*, and then became curiously agitated. She rose and looked at her face in the small silverframed mirror. Yes, there were lines, but faint still, and natural. Her nails needed filing. She decided to change into a shirt and jeans and then to rearrange all her clothes and jewellery. A week, two weeks, passed in this way. She got nothing written. The early sense of calm and order left her.

She saw one person fairly constantly during that time, a local *guardia* whose name was Manolo. He had first come to the house with a telegram from her old theatre, asking her if she would do a translation of a play of Mayakovsky's for them. She offered him a drink when he came with the telegram. He asked for water, and later he walked with her back to the village where she cabled her acceptance of the theatre's offer, wheeling his rattling bicycle, the thin glittering barrel of his rifle pointed skyward. The Russian manuscript of the play arrived by express delivery a few days afterwards, and now she spent all her mornings working on the translation; and how easy it was, the good text solidly and reliably under her hand: it was play compared with the pain of trying to pluck the life of Chekhov out of the unimaginable air.

Manolo began to come almost daily, in the hot lazy three or four of the afternoon. She could hear his boots scrape noisily on the gravel to give her warning. He would leave his bicycle against the wall of the house in the shade, his gun where the drinking water dripped slowly from the porous clay jars into catching pails. They would talk for an hour or more across the bare Scandinavian table, and he would smoke and drink wine or water. His talk turned often to the social ills of Spain and the impossibility of the natural division between men and women. She wondered why someone as intelligent as he could have become a *guardia*. There was nothing else to do, he told her: he was one of the lucky ones in the village, he got a salary, it was that or Germany. And then he married, and bang-bang, he said—two babies in less than two years. A third was on its way. All his wife's time was taken up with the infants now. There was nothing left between them but babies, and that was the way it would go on, without any money, seven or eleven or more. . . .

'But that's criminal in this age,' she said.

'What is there to do?'

'There's contraception.'

'In Spain there's not.'

'They could be brought in.'

'Could you get some in? If you could I'd pay you,' he said eagerly, and when she sent back the completed translation she asked the theatre's editor if he could send the contraceptives with the next commission. She explained why she wanted them, though she reflected that he would think what he wanted anyhow. The contraceptives did get through with the next commissioned play. They wanted a new translation of *The Seagull*, which delighted her; she felt it would bring her closer to her Chekhov and that when she had finished it she would be able to begin what she had come here to try to do in the first place. The only objection the editor had to sending the contraceptives was that he was uneasy for her safety: it was against the law, and it was Spain, and policemen were as notorious as other people for wanting promotion. She thought Manolo was nervous and he left her quickly after she handed him the package that afternoon, but she put it out of mind as natural embarrassment in taking contraceptives from a woman, and went back to reading *The Seagull*. She was still reading it and making notes towards her translation on the margins when she heard boots and voices coming up the gravel, and a loud knock with what sounded like a gun butt came on the door. She was frightened as she called out, 'Who's there?' and a voice she didn't know called back, 'Open. It's the police.' When she opened the door she saw Manolo and the *jefe* of the local *guardia*, a fat oily man she had often seen lolling about the market, and he at once barged into the house. Manolo closed the door behind them as she instinctively got behind the table.

The *jefe* threw the package she had given Manolo earlier in the day on to the table. 'You know this?' and as she nodded she noticed in growing fear that both of them were very drunk. 'You know it's against the law? You can go to prison for this,' he said, the small oily eyes glittering across the table, and she decided there was no use answering any more.

'Still, Manolo and myself have agreed to forget it if we can try them out here,' his oily eyes fell pointedly on the package

24

on the table but the voice was hesitant. 'That's if you don't prefer it Spanish style,' he laughed back to Manolo for support, and
started to edge round the table.

They were drunk and excited. They would probably take her
anyhow. How often had she heard this problem argued. Usually
it was agreed that it was better to yield than to get hurt. After
all, sex wasn't all it was cracked up to be: in Paris the butcher
and the baker shook hands with the local whore when they met,
as people simply plying different trades.

'All right. As long as you promise to leave as soon as it's
done,' her voice stopped him, it had a calm she didn't feel.

'Okay, it's a promise,' they both nodded eagerly, and they
reminded her of mastered boys as they asked apprehensively,
'With the . . . or without?'

'With.'

The *jefe* followed her first into the room. 'All the clothes
off,' was his one demand, and she complied. She averted her
face sideways while it took place. A few times after parties
when she was younger hadn't she held almost total strangers
in her arms? Then she fixed completely on the two sentences
*The word Oysters was chalked on the wagon that carried Chek-
hov's body to Moscow for burial. The coffin was carried in the
oyster wagon because of the fierce heat of early July,* her mind
moving over them from beginning to end, and from beginning
to end, again and again. Manolo rushed out of the room when
he had finished. They kept their word and left, subdued and
quiet. It had not been as jolly as they must have imagined it
would be.

  She showered and washed and changed into new clothes. She
poured herself a large glass of cognac at the table, noticing that
they must have taken the condoms with them, and then began
to sob, dry and hard at first, rising to a flood of rage against her
own foolishness. 'There is only one real sin—stupidity. You
always get punished for behaving stupidly,' the poet Severi was
fond of repeating.

25

When she quietened she drank what was left of the cognac and then started to pack. She stayed up all night packing and putting the house in order for her departure. Numbed with tiredness she walked to the village the next morning. All the seats on the express that passed through Vera were booked for that day but she could take the *rápido* to Granada and go straight to Barcelona from there. She arranged for the one taxi in the village to take her to the train. The taximan came and she made listless replies to his ebullient talk on the drive by the sea to meet the train. The *rápido* was full of peasants and as it crawled from station to small station she knew it would be night before it reached Granada. She would find some hotel close to the station. In the morning she would see a doctor and then go to Barcelona. A woman in a black shawl on the wooden seat facing her offered her a sliver of sausage and a gourd of wine. She took the sausage but refused the wine as she wasn't confident that her hands were steady enough to direct the thin stream into her mouth. Then she nodded to sleep, and when she woke she thought the bitter taste of oysters was in her mouth and that an awful lot of people were pacing up and down and waving their arms around, and she had a sudden desire to look out the window to see if the word *Oysters* was chalked on the wagon; but then she saw that the train had just stopped at a large station and that the woman in the black shawl was still there and was smiling on her.

A Slip-up

There was such a strain on the silence between them after he'd eaten that it had to be broken.

'Maybe we should never have given up the farm and come here. Even though we had no one to pass it on to,' Michael said, his head of coarse white hair leaning away from his wife as he spoke. What had happened today would never have happened if they'd stayed, he thought, and there'd be no shame; but he did not speak it.

'Racing across hedges and ditches after cattle, is it, at our age. Cows, hens, pigs, calves, racing from light to dark on those watery fields between two lakes, up to the tips of our wellingtons in mud and water, having to run with the deeds to the bank manager after a bad year. I thought we'd gone into all this before.'

'Well, we'd never have had to retire if we'd stayed'; what he said already sounded lame.

'We'd be retired all right. We'd be retired all right, into the graveyard long years ago if we'd stayed. You don't know what a day this has been for me as well,' Agnes began to cry and Michael sat still in the chair as she cried.

'After I came home from Tesco's I sorted the parcels,' she said. 'And at ten to one I put the kippers under the grill. Michael will have just about finished his bottle of Bass and be coming out the door of the Royal, I said when I looked at the clock. Michael must have run into someone on his way back, I thought, as it went past one. And when it got to ten past I said you must have fell in with company, but I was beginning to get worried.'

'You know I never fall in with company,' he protested irritably. 'I always leave the Royal at ten to, never a minute more nor less.'

'I didn't know what way to turn when it got to half past, I was that paralysed with worry, and then I said I'll wait five minutes to see, and five minutes, and another five minutes, and I·wasn't able to move with worry, and then it was nearly a quarter past two. I couldn't stand it. And then I said I'll go down to the Royal. And I'll never know why I didn't think of it before.

'Denis and Joan were just beginning to lock up when I got to the Royal. "What is it, Agnes?" Denis said, "Have you seen Michael?" I asked. "No," Denis shook his head. "He hasn't been in at all today. We were wondering if he was all right. It's the first time he's not showed up for his bottle of Bass since he had that flu last winter." "He's not showed up for his lunch either and he's always on the dot. What can have happened to him?" I started to cry.

'Joan made me sit down. Denis put a brandy with a drop of port in it into my hand. After I'd taken a sip he said, "When did you last see Michael?" I told him how we went to Tesco's, and how I thought you'd gone for your bottle of Bass, and how I put on the kippers, and how you never showed up. Joan took out a glass of beer and sat with me while Denis got on the phone. "Don't worry, Agnes," Joan said, "Denis is finding out about Michael." And when Denis got off the phone he said, "He's not in any of the hospitals and the police haven't got him so he must be all right. Don't rush the brandy. As soon as you finish we'll hop in the car. He must be nearhand."

'We drove all round the park but you weren't on any of the benches. "What'll we do now?" I said. "Before we do anything we'll take a quick scout round the streets," Denis said, and as soon as we went through the lights before Tesco's he said, "Isn't that Michael over there with the shopping bag?"

'And there you were, with the empty shopping bag in front

of Tesco's window. "Oh my God," I said, "Michael will kill me. I must have forgot to collect him when I came out of Tesco's," and then Denis blew the horn, and you saw us, and came over.'

Every morning since he retired, except when he was down with that winter flu, Michael walked with Agnes to Tesco's, and it brought him the feeling of long ago when he walked round the lake with his mother, potholes and stones of the lane, the boat shapes at intervals in the long lake wall to allow the carts to pass one another when they met, the oilcloth shopping bag he carried for her in a glow of chattering as he walked in the shelter of her shadow. Now it was Agnes who chattered as they walked to Tesco's, and he'd no longer to listen, any response to her bead of talk had long become nothing but an irritation to her; and so he walked safe in the shelter of those dead days, drawing closer to the farm between the lakes that they had lost.

When they reached Tesco's he did not go in. The brands and bright lights troubled him, and as she made all the purchases he had no function within anyhow. So on dry days he stayed outside with the empty shopping bag if it wasn't too cold. When the weather was miserable he waited for her just inside the door beside the off-licence counter. When he first began to come with her after retiring, the off-licence assistants used to bother him by asking if they could help. As he said, 'No thanks,' he wanted to tell them that he never drank in the house. Only at Christmas did they have drink in the house. And that was for other people, if they came. The last bottles were now three Christmases old, for people no longer visited them at Christmas, which was far more convenient. They went round to the Royal as usual Christmas Day. Denis still kept Sunday hours Christmas Day in the Royal. Though it was only the new assistants in the off-licence who ever noticed him on bad days now, he still preferred to wait for her outside with the shopping bag against

the Special Offers pasted in the glass. By that time he would
have already reached the farm between the lakes while walking
with her, and was ready for work. The farm that they lost when
they came to London he'd won back almost completely since he
retired. He'd been dismayed when he retired as caretaker of the
Sir John Cass School to find how much the farm had run down
in the years he'd been a school caretaker. Drains were choked.
The fields were full of rushes. The garden had gone wild, and
the hedges were invading the fields. But he was too old a hand
to rush at things. Each day he set himself a single task. The
stone wall was his pride, perhaps because it was the beginning.
Before the wall was built there were no limits. Everything
looked impossible. A hundred hands seemed needed. But after
the wall was built he cleared the weeds and bushes that had
overgrown the front garden, cut away the egg bushes from the
choked whitethorns, pruned the whitethorns so that they
thickened. Now between wall and whitethorn hedge the front
garden ran, and he'd gone out from there, task by single
task.

This morning as he walked with Agnes he decided to clear
the drinking pool which was dry after the long spell of good
weather. First he shovelled the dark earth of rotted leaves and
cowshit out on the bank. Then he paved the sides with heavy
stones so that the cattle would not plough in as they drank,
and he cleared the weeds from the small stream that fed it.
When he followed the stream to the boundary hedge he found
water blocked there. He released it and then leaned on his
shovel in the simple pleasure of watching water flow. For all
that time he was unaware of the shopping bag, but when all the
water had flowed down towards the pool he felt it again by his
side. He wondered what was keeping Agnes. He'd never finished
such a long job before outside Tesco's. Usually he'd counted
himself lucky if he was through with such a job by the time he'd
finished his bottle of Bass in the Royal by ten to one.

The drain was now empty and clean. All the water had flowed

down to the pool. He'd go to the field garden. The withered
bean and pea stalks needed pulling up, and the earth turned.
A wren or robin sang in the thorns, faithful still in the bare days.
He opened the wooden gate into the garden, enclosed on three
sides by its natural thorn hedges, and two strands of barbed
wire ran on posts to keep the cattle out on the fourth. Each year
he pushed the barbed wire farther out, and soon, one of these
years, the whole field would be a garden, completely enclosed by
its own whitethorns. He pulled up the withered bean and pea
stalks with the thorn branches that had served as stakes and
threw them in a heap for burning. Then he began to turn the
soil. The black and white bean flower had been his favourite,
its fragrance carried on the wind through the thorns into the
meadow, drawing the bees from the clover. Agnes could keep all
her roses in the front garden . . . and then he felt himself
leaning over the fork with tiredness, though he hadn't half the
ridge turned. He was too weak to work. It must be late and
why had she not called him to his meal? He stuck the fork in
the ground and in exasperation went over to the barbed wire.
The strands were loose. A small alder shoot sprouted from one
of the posts. He walked up the potato furrows, the dried stalks
dead and grey on the ridges. This year he must move the pit
to higher ground, for last winter the rats had come up from the
lake, but why had she not called him? Had she no care? Was
she so utterly selfish?

He turned and stared in the window, but the avenues of
shelves were too long and the lights blinding. It was in this
impotent rage that he heard the horn blow. Denis was there,
and Agnes was in the car. He went towards them with the empty
shopping bag. They both got out of the car.

'Why did you leave me there?' he asked angrily.

'Oh don't be mad at me, Michael. I must have forgot when
I came out.'

'What time is it now?'

'Five after three, Michael,' Dennis was smiling. 'You've missed your bottle of Bass, but hop in and I'll run you home.'

'It wouldn't have happened if we'd kept the farm. At least on the farm we'd be away from people,' he thought obstinately as he put the food aside that he should have eaten hours before. He flushed as a child with shame as he heard again, 'Five after three, Michael. You've missed your bottle of Bass, but hop in and I'll run you home,' and thought that's how it goes, you go on as usual every day, and then something happens, and you make a mistake, and you're caught. It was Agnes who at last broke this impossible silence.

'I can see that you're tired out. Why don't you lie down for a turn?' she said, and began to clear the plates.

'Maybe I will lie down then,' he yielded.

He slept lightly and restlessly. Only a fraction of what was happening surfaced in his dream. A herd of panting cattle was driven past him on a dirt road by a man wheeling a bicycle, their mouths slavering in the heat. Agnes passed by holding bread-crumbs in her apron. A white car came round the lake. As it turned at the gate a child got out and came towards him with a telegram. He was fumbling in his pocket for coins to give to the child when he was woken by Agnes.

'We'll be late getting to the Royal if you don't get up now,' she was saying.

'What time is it?'

When she told him the time he knew they should be leaving in twenty minutes.

'I don't know if I want to go out tonight.'

'Of course you'll go out tonight. There's nothing wrong with you, is there?'

When she said that he knew he had to go. He rose and washed, changed into his suit, combed his coarse white hair, and at exactly twenty to nine, as on every evening of their lives, they were closing the 37B door in Ainsworth Road behind them.

All the saloon regulars looked unusually happy and bright as they greeted the old couple in the Royal; and when Michael proffered the coins for the Guinness and pint of Bass, Denis pushed them away. 'They're on the house tonight, Michael. You have to make up for that missed bottle of Bass tonight.'

Blindly he carried the drinks towards Agnes at the table. When he turned and sat and faced the room with his raised glass the whole saloon rang with, 'Cheers, Agnes. Cheers, Michael.'

'You see it was all in your mind, Michael. Everybody's the same as usual. Even happier,' Agnes said afterwards in the quiet of the click of billiard balls coming from the Public Bar.

'Maybe. Maybe, Agnes,' Michael drank.

All the people were elated too on the small farms around the lakes for weeks after Fraser Woods had tried to hang himself from a branch of an apple tree in his garden, the unconcealed excitement in their voices as they said, 'Isn't it terrible what happened to poor Fraser?' and the lust on their faces as they waited for their excitement to be mirrored.

'We'll go early to Tesco's in the morning. And then you can come down for your bottle of Bass. And it'll be the same as if nothing ever happened. What was it anyhow?' Agnes said, warmed by the Guinness.

'I suppose it was just a slip-up,' Michael answered as he sipped slowly at his pint, trying to put off the time when he'd have to go up to the counter for their next round.

All Sorts of Impossible Things

They were out coursing on Sunday a last time together but they did not know it, the two friends, James Sharkey and Tom Lennon, a teacher and an agricultural instructor. The weak winter sun had thawed the fields soft enough to course the hare on, and though it still hung blood-orange above the hawthorns on the hill the rims of the hoof tracks were already hardening fast against their tread.

The hounds walked beside them on slip leashes: a pure-bred fawn bitch that had raced under the name of Coolcarra Queen, reaching the Final of the Rockingham Stakes the season before; and a wire-haired mongrel, no more than half-hound, that the schoolmaster, James Sharkey, borrowed from Charlie's bar for these Sundays. They'd been beating up the bottoms for some hours, and odd snipe, exploding out of the rushes before zigzagging away, was all that had risen.

'If we don't rise something before long we'll soon have to throw our hats at it,' Tom Lennon said, and it was a careless phrase. No one had seen the teacher without his eternal brown hat for the past twenty years. 'I've been noticing the ground harden all right,' the dry answer came.

'Anyhow, I'm beginning to feel a bit humped,' Tom Lennon looked small and frail in the tightly belted white raincoat.

'There's no use rimming it, then. There'll be other Sundays.'

Suddenly a large hare rose ahead, bounded to the edge of the rushes, and then looped high to watch and listen. With a 'Hulla, hulla,' they slipped the hounds, the hare racing for the side of the hill. The fawn bitch led, moving in one beautiful killing line as she closed with the hare, the head eel-like as it struck;

but the hare twisted away from the teeth, and her speed carried the fawn past. The hare had to turn again a second time as the mongrel coming up from behind tried to pick it in the turn. The two men below in the rushes watched in silence as the old dance played itself out on the bare side of the hill: race, turn, race again; the hounds hunting well together, the mongrel making up with cunning what he lacked in grace, pacing himself to strike when the hare was most vulnerable—turning back from the fawn. But with every fresh turn the hare gained, the hounds slithering past on the hard ground. They were utterly beaten by the time the hare left them, going away through the hedge of whitethorns.

'They picked a warrior there.'

'That's for sure,' Tom Lennon answered as quietly.

The beaten hounds came disconsolately down, pausing at the foot of the hill to lap water from a wheelmark and to lick their paws. They came on towards the men. The paws were bleeding and some of the bitch's nails were broken.

'Maybe we shouldn't have raced her on such hard ground,' the teacher said by way of apology.

'That's no difference. She'll never run in the Stakes again. They say there's only two kinds to have—a proper dud or a champion. Her kind, the in-between, are the very worst. They'll always run well enough to tempt you into having another go. Anyhow, there's not the money for that any more,' he said with a sad smile of reflection.

Coolcarra Queen was a relic of his bachelor days that he hadn't been able to bear parting with on getting married and first coming to the place as temporary agricultural instructor.

They'd raced her in the Stakes. She'd almost won. They'd trained her together, turn and turn about. And that cold wet evening, the light failing as they ran off the Finals, they'd stood together in the mud beside the net of torn hares and watched this hare escape into the laurels that camouflaged the

36

pen, and the judge gallop towards the rope on the old fat horse, and stop, and lift the white kerchief instead of the red. Coolcarra Queen had lost the Rockingham Silver Cup and twenty-five pounds after winning the four races that had taken her to the Final.

'Still, she gave us a run for our money,' the teacher said as they put the limping hounds on the leashes and turned home.

'Well, it's over now,' Tom Lennon said. 'Especially with the price of steak.'

'Your exams can't be far off now?' the teacher said as they walked. The exams he alluded to were to determine whether the instructor should be made permanent or let go.

'In less than five weeks. The week after Easter.'

'Are you anxious about it all?'

'Of course,' he said sadly. 'If they make me permanent I get paid whether I'm sick or well. They can't get rid of me then. Temporary is only all right while you're single.'

'Do you foresee any snags?'

'Not in the exams. I know as much as they'll know. It's the medical I'm afraid of.'

'Still,' the teacher began lamely and couldn't go on. He knew that the instructor had been born with his heart on the wrong side and it was weak.

'Not that they'll pay much heed to instruction round here. Last week I came on a pair of gentlemen during my rounds. They'd roped a horse-mower to a brand new Ferguson. One was driving the Ferguson, the other sitting up behind on the horse machine, lifting and letting down the blade with a piece of wire. They were cutting thistles.'

'That's the form all right,' the teacher smiled.

They'd left the fields and had come to the stone bridge into the village. Only one goalpost stood upright in the football field. Below them the sluggish Shannon flowed between its wheaten reeds.

37

'Still, we must have walked a good twelve miles today from one field to the next. While if we'd to walk that distance along a straight line of road it'd seem a terrible journey.'

'A bit like life itself,' the teacher laughed sarcastically, adjusting the brown hat firmly on his head. 'We might never manage it if we had to take it all in the one gasp. We mightn't even manage to finish it.'

'Well, it'd be finished for us then,' the instructor countered weakly.

'Do you feel like coming to Charlie's for a glass?' he asked as they stood.

'I told her I'd be back for the dinner. If I'm in time for the dinner she might have something even better for me afterwards,' Tom Lennon joked defensively.

'She might indeed. Well, I have to take this towser back to Charlie anyhow. Thanks for the day.'

'Thanks yourself,' Tom Lennon said.

Above the arms of the stone wall the teacher watched the frail little instructor turn up the avenue towards the Bawn, a straggling rectangular building partly visible through the bare trees, where he had rooms in the tower, all that was left of the old Hall.

Charlie was on his stool behind the bar with the Sunday paper when the teacher came with the mongrel through the partition. Otherwise the bar and shop were empty.

'Did yous catch anything?' he yawned as he put aside the paper, drawing the back of his hands over his eyes like a child. There was a dark stain of hair oil behind him on the whitewash where sometimes he leaned his head and slept when the bar was empty.

'We roused only one and he slipped them.'

'I'm thinking there's only the warriors left by this time of year,' he laughed, and when he laughed the tip of his red nose curled up in a way that caused the teacher to smile with affection.

'I suppose I'll let the old towser out the back?'

Charlie nodded. 'I'll get one of the children to throw him some food later.' When the door was closed again he said in a hushed, solicitous voice, 'I suppose, Master, it'll be whiskey?'

'A large one, Charlie,' the teacher said.

In a delicious glow of tiredness from the walking, and the sensuous burning of the whiskey as it went down, he was almost mindless in the shuttle back and forth of talk until he saw Charlie go utterly still. He was following each move his wife made at the other end of the house. The face was beautiful in its concentration, reflecting each move or noise she made as clearly as water will the drifting clouds. When he was satisfied that there was no sudden danger of her coming up to the bar he turned to the shelves. Though the teacher could not see past the broad back, he had witnessed the little subterfuge so often that he could follow it in exact detail: the silent unscrewing of the bottle cap, the quick tip of the whiskey into the glass, the silent putting back of the cap, and the downing of the whiskey in one gulp, the movements so practised that it took but seconds. Coughing violently, he turned and ran the water and drank the glass of water into the coughing. While he waited for the coughing to die, he rearranged bottles on the shelves. The teacher was so intimate with the subterfuge that he might as well have taken part in the act of murder or of love. 'If I'm home in time for the dinner she might have something even better for me afterwards,' he remembered with resentment.

'Tom didn't come with you?' Charlie asked as soon as he brought the fit of coughing under control.

'No. He was done in with the walking and the wife was expecting him.'

'They say he's coming up for permanent soon. Do you think he will have any trouble?'

'The most thing he's afraid of is the medical.'

Charlie was silent for a while, and then he said, 'It's a quare caper that, isn't it, the heart on the wrong side?'

'There's many a quare caper, Charlie,' the teacher replied. 'Life itself is a quare caper if you ask me.'

'But what'll he do if he doesn't get permanent?'

'What'll we all do, Charlie?' the teacher said inwardly, and as always when driven in to reflect on his own life, instinctively fixed the brown hat more firmly on his head.

Once he did not bother to wear a hat or a cap over his thick curly fair hair even when it was raining. And he was in love then with Cathleen O'Neill. They'd thought time would wait for them forever as they went to the sea in his baby Austin or to dances after spending Sundays on the river. And then, suddenly, his hair began to fall out. Anxiety exasperated desire to a passion, the passion to secure his life as he felt it all slip away, to moor it to the woman he loved. Now it was her turn to linger. She would not marry him and she would not let him go.

'Will you marry me or not? I want an answer one way or the other this evening.' He felt his whole life like a stone on the edge of a boat out on water.

'What if I don't want to answer?' They were both proud and iron-willed.

'Then I'll take it as No.'

'You'll have to take it whatever way you want, then.' Her face was flushed with resentment.

'Goodbye, then.' He steeled himself to turn away.

Twice he almost paused but no voice calling him back came. At the open iron gate above the stream he did pause. 'If I cross it here it is the end. Anything is better than the anguish of uncertainty. If I cross here I cannot turn back even if she should want.' He counted till ten, and looked back, but her back was turned, walking slowly uphill to the house. As she passed through the gate he felt a tearing that broke as an inaudible cry.

No one ever saw him afterwards without his brown hat, and there was great scandal the first Sunday he wore it in the body of the church. The man kneeling next to him nudged him, gestured with his thumb at the hat, but the teacher did not even move. Whispers and titters and one hysterical whinny of laughter that set off a general sneeze ran through the congregation as he unflinchingly wore it through the service.

The priest was up to the school just before hometime the very next day. They let the children home early.

'Have you seen Miss O'Neill recently, Jim?' the priest opened cautiously, for he liked the young teacher, the most intelligent and competent he had.

'No, Father. That business is finished.'

'There'd be no point in me putting in a word?'

'There'd be no point, Father.'

'I'm sorry to hear that. It's no surprise. Everything gets round these parts in a shape.'

'In a shape, certainly, Father.' There was dry mockery in the voice.

'When it gets wild it is different, when you hear talk of nothing else—and that's what has brought me up. What's going the rounds now is that you wore your hat all through Mass yesterday.'

'They were right for once, Father.'

'I'm amazed.'

'Why, Father?'

'You're an intelligent man. You know you can't do that, Jim.'

'Why not, Father?'

'You don't need me to tell you that it'd appear as an extreme form of disrespect.'

'If the church can't include my own old brown hat, it can't include very much, can it, Father?'

'You know that and I know that, but we both know that the

41

outward shows may least belie themselves. It'd not be tolerated.'

'It'll have to be tolerated, Father, or . . .'

'You can't be that mad. I know you're the most intelligent man round here.'

'Thanks, Father. All votes in that direction count round here. "They said I was mad and I said they were mad, and confound them they outvoted me," ' he quoted. 'That's about it, isn't it, Father?'

'Ah, stop it, Jim. Tell me why. Seriously, tell me why.'

'You may have noticed recently, Father,' he began slowly, in rueful mockery, 'a certain manifestation that my youth is ended. Namely, that I'm almost bald. It had the effect of *timor mortis*. So I decided to cover it up.'

'Many lose their hair. Bald or grey, what does it matter? We all go that way.'

'So?'

'When I look down from the altar on Sunday half the heads on the men's side are bald.'

'The women must cover their crowning glory and the men must expose their lack of a crown. So that's the old church in her wisdom bringing us all to heel?'

'I can't understand all this fooling, Jim.'

'I'm deadly serious. I'll wear my hat in the same way as you wear your collar, Father.'

'But that's nonsense. It's completely different.'

'Your collar is the sublimation of *timor mortis*, what else is it, in Jesus Christ. All I'm asking is to cover it up.'

'But you can't wear it all the time?'

'Maybe not in bed but that's different.'

'Listen. This joking has gone far enough. I don't care where you wear your hat. That's your problem. But if you wear it in church you make it my problem.'

'Well, you'll have to do something about it then, Father.'

The priest went very silent but when he spoke all he said was:

'Why don't we lock up the school? We can walk down the road together.'

What faced the priest was alarmingly simple: he couldn't have James Sharkey at Mass with his hat on and he couldn't have one of his teachers not at Sunday Mass. Only late that night did a glimmer of what might be done come to him. Every second Sunday the teacher collected coins from the people entering the church at a table just inside the door. If the collection table was moved out to the porch and Sharkey agreed to collect the coins every Sunday, perhaps he could still make his observances while keeping his infernal hat on. The next morning he went to the administrator.

'By luck we seem to have hit on a solution,' he was able to explain to the teacher that evening.

'That's fine with me. I never wanted to be awkward,' the teacher said.

'You never wanted to be awkward,' the priest exploded. 'You should have heard me trying to convince the administrator this morning that it was better to move the table out into the porch than to move you out of the school. I've never seen a man so angry in my life. You'd have got short shrift, I'm telling you, if you were in his end of the parish. Tell me, tell me what would you have done if the administrator had got his way and fired you?'

'I'd have got by somehow. Others do,' he answered.

And soon people had got so used to the gaunt face under the brown hat behind the collection table every Sunday that they'd be as shocked now to see him without it after all the years as they had been on the first Sunday he wore it.

'That's right, Charlie. What'll we all do?' he repeated as he finished the whiskey beside the oil heater. 'Here. Give us another drop before the crowd start to come in and I get caught.'

'My brown hat and his heart on the wrong side, and you tippling away secretly when the whole parish including your wife knows it. It's a quare caper indeed, Charlie,' he thought as he quickly finished his whiskey to avoid getting caught by the crowd due to come in.

There was no more coursing together again after that Sunday. The doctor's car was parked a long time outside the white gate that led to the Bawn the next day, and when Tom Lennon's old Ford wasn't seen around the roads that day or the next or the next the teacher went to visit him, taking a half-bottle of whiskey. Lennon's young wife, a warm soft country girl of few words, let him in.

'How is he?' he asked.

'The doctor'll be out again tomorrow,' she answered timidly and led him up the creaky narrow stairs. 'He'll be delighted to see you. He gets depressed not being able to be up and about.'

From the circular room of the tower that they used as a living room he could hear happy gurgles of the baby as they climbed the stairs, and as soon as she showed him into the bedroom she left. In the pile of bedclothes Tom Lennon looked smaller and more frail than he usually did.

'How is the patient?'

'Fed up,' he said. 'It's great to see a face after staring all day at the ceiling.'

'What is it?'

'The old ticker. As soon as I'd eaten after getting home on Sunday it started playing me up. Maybe I overdid the walking. Still, it could be worse. It'd be a damned sight worse if it had happened in five weeks' time. Then we'd be properly in the soup.'

'You have oodles of time to be fit for the exam,' the teacher said, hiding his dismay by putting the whiskey down on the dressing table. 'I brought this little something.' There was, he felt, a bloom of death in the room.

'You never know,' the instructor said some hours later as the teacher took his leave. 'I'm hoping the doctor'll have me up to-morrow.' He'd drunk only a little of the whiskey in a punch his wife had made, while the hatted man on the chair slowly finished his own half-bottle neat.

The doctor did not allow him up that week or the next, and the teacher began to come every evening to the house, and two Sundays later he asked to take the hounds out on his own. He did not cross the bridge to the Plains as they'd done the Sunday together but went along the river to Doireen. The sedge of the long lowlands rested wheaten and dull between two hills of hazel and briar in the warm day. All winter it had been flooded but the pale dead grass now crackled under his feet like tinder. He beat along the edges of the hills, feeling that the hares might have come out of the scrub to sleep in the sun, and as he beat he began to feel Tom Lennon's absence like his own lengthening shadow on the pale sedge.

The first hare didn't get more than halfway from where it was lying to the cover of the scrub before the fawn's speed caught it, a flash of white belly fur as it rolled over, not being able to turn away from the teeth in the long sedge, and the terror of its crying as both hounds tore it began. He wrested the hare loose and stilled the weird child-like crying with one blow. Soon afterwards a second hare fell in the same way. From several parts of the river lowland he saw hares looping slowly out of the warm sun into the safety of the scrub. He knew they'd all have gone in then, and he turned back for Charlie's. He gave one of the hares to Charlie; the other he skinned and took with him to Tom Lennon's.

'Do you know what I'm thinking?' he said that night. 'I'm thinking that I should take the bitch.'

He saw sudden fear in the sick man's eyes.

'You know you're always welcome to borrow her any time you want.'

'It's not that,' he said quickly. 'I thought just to take her until you're better. I could feed her. It'd be no trouble. It'd take some of the weight off the wife.' And that evening when he left he took the bitch who was excited, thinking that she was going hunting again, though it was dark, and she rose to put paws on his shoulders and to lick his face.

She settled in easily with the teacher. He made a house for her out of a scrapped Ford in the garden but he still let her sleep in the house, and there was a lighter spring in his walk each evening he left school, knowing the excitement with which he would be met as soon as he got home. At night he listened to Tom Lennon's increasingly feverish grumblings as the exam drew closer. And he looked so angry and ill the night after the doctor had told him he could put all thought of the exam out of his mind that the suspicion grew stronger in the teacher's mind that his friend might not after all be just ill.

'What are you going to do?' he asked fearfully.

'Do the exam, of course.' There was determination as well as fear in the sunken eyes.

'But you can't do it if the doctor said you weren't fit.'

'Let's put it this way,' the sick man laughed in harsh triumph, 'I can't *not* do it.'

The night before the exam he asked the teacher to bring up the clippers. He wanted a haircut. And that night as the teacher wrapped the towel round the instructor's neck and took the bright clippers out of their pale green cardboard box, adjusting the combs, and started to clip, the black hair dribbling down on the towel, he felt for the first time ever a mad desire to remove his hat and stand bareheaded in the room, as if for the first time in years he felt himself in the presence of something sacred.

'That's a great job,' Tom Lennon said afterwards. 'You know while we're at it, I might as well go the whole hog, and shave as well.'

'Do you want me to get you some hot water?'

'That wouldn't be too much trouble?'

'No trouble at all.'

Downstairs as they waited for the water to boil, the wife in her quiet voice asked him, 'What do you think?'

'He seems determined on it. I tried to talk him out of it but it was no use.'

'No. It doesn't seem any use,' she said. A starched white shirt and blue suit and tie were draped across a chair one side of the fire.

The teacher sat on the bed's edge and held the bowl of water steady while the instructor shaved. When he finished, he examined himself carefully in the little hand-mirror, and joked, 'It's as good as for a wedding.'

'Maybe it's too risky. Maybe you should send in a certificate. There'll be another chance.'

'No. That's finished. I'm going through with it. It's my last chance. There'll be no other chance. If I manage to get made permanent there'd be a weight off my mind and it'd be better than a hundred doctors and tonics.'

'Maybe I should give the old car a swing in readiness for the morning, so?'

'That'd be great.' The instructor fumbled for his car keys in his trouser pockets on the bed rail.

The engine was cold but started on the sixth or seventh swing. In the cold starlit night he stood and listened to the engine run.

'Good luck, old Tom,' he said quietly as he switched it off and took the car keys in.

'Well, good luck tomorrow. I hope all goes well. I'll be up as soon as I see the car back to find out how it went,' he said in a singsong voice he used with the children at school in order not to betray his emotion after telling him that the Ford was running like a bird.

Tom Lennon rose the next morning as he said he would, dressed in his best clothes, had tea, told his wife not to worry and that he'd be back about six, somehow got as far as the car, and fell dead over the starting handle the teacher had left in the engine from the previous night.

When word was brought to the school, all the hatted man did was bow his head and murmur, 'Thanks.' He knew he had been expecting the death for some days. And when he went to the Bawn a last time he felt no terror of the stillness of the brown habit, the folded hands, but only a certain amazement that it was the agricultural instructor who was lying there not he. Two days later his hat stood calmly among the scarved women and bareheaded men about the open grave, and when it was over he went back to Charlie's. The bar was filled with mourners from the funeral-making holiday. A silence seemed to fall as the brown hat came through the partition, but only for a moment. They were arguing about a method of sowing winter wheat that the dead man used to advocate. Some thought it made sense. Others said it would turn out to be a disaster.

'Your old friend won't hunt again,' Charlie said as he handed him the whiskey. The voice was hushed. The eyes stared inquiringly but respectfully into the gaunt face beneath the hat. The small red curl of the nose was still.

'No. He'll not hunt again.'

'They say herself and the child is going home with her own people this evening. They'll send a van up later for the furniture.' His voice was low as a whisper at the corner of the bar.

'That makes sense,' the teacher said.

'You have the bitch still?' Charlie asked.

'That's right. I'll be glad to keep her, but the wife may want to take her with her.'

'That'll be the least of her troubles. She'll not want.'

"Will you have something yourself?' the teacher invited.

'All right then, Master,' he paused suddenly. 'A quick one then. We all need a little something in the open today,' and he smiled an apologetic, rueful smile in his small eyes; but he downed the whiskey, as quickly running a glass of water and drinking it into the coughing, as if it hadn't been in the open at all.

The fawn jumped in her excitement on her new master when he finally came home from the funeral. As he petted her down, gripping her neck, bringing his own face down to hers, thinking how he had come by her, he felt the same rush of feeling as he had felt when he watched the locks of hair fall on to the towel round the neck in the room; but instead of prayer he now felt a wild longing to throw his hat away and walk round the world bareheaded, find some girl, not necessarily Cathleen O'Neill, but any young girl, and go to the sea with her as he used to, leave the car at the harbour wall and take the boat for the island, the engine beating like a good heart under the deck boards as the waves rocked it on turning out of the harbour, hold her in one long embrace all night between the hotel sheets; or train the fawn again, feed her the best steak from town, walk her four miles every day for months, stand in the mud and rain again and see her as Coolcarra Queen race through the field in the Rockingham Stakes, see the judge gallop over to the rope on the old fat horse, and this time lift high the red kerchief to give the Silver Cup to Coolcarra Queen.

And until he calmed, and went into the house, his mind raced with desire for all sorts of such impossible things.

Faith, Hope and Charity

Cunningham and Murphy had worked as a team ever since they'd met on a flyover site outside Reading. They dug trenches and were paid by the yard. The trenches were in places where machines could not easily go, and the work was dangerous, the earth walls having to be shuttered up as they went along, the shutters held apart by metal bars with adjustable flat squares on both ends. Both men worked under assumed names to avoid paying income tax.

This money that they slaved for all the year in the trenches they flashed and wasted in one royal month each summer in Ireland. As men obsessed with the idea that all knowledge lies within a woman's body, but having entered it to find themselves as ignorant as before, they are driven towards all women again and again: in childish hope that somehow the next time they will find the treasure, and then the equally childish desire for revenge since it cannot be found, that knife in the unfathomable entrails; and they grow full of hatred. Each year, as Murphy and Cunningham dug in the trench towards their next royal summer, their talk grew obsessional and more bitter. 'It's a kind of a sort of a country that can't even afford a national eejit so they all have to take turns,' they'd say and laugh harshly.

What slowed them up the most was not the digging but the putting up of the shuttering behind them. And as August drew close they grew careless as their greed for money grew, in order to make an even bigger splash this summer than ever before. Little by little the spaces between the metal bars lengthened. Like all stupid people they felt themselves invulnerable: no

51

matter how careless they were the bad accident was bound to happen elsewhere.

Murphy was standing on top of the trench watching Cunningham wield the pick below, behind him the fence of split stakes on Hessell Street. The midday sun beat mercilessly down on the trench, and they worked it turn and turn about, coming up every five minutes or so to cool in whatever air stirred from the Thames.

The only warning the trench gave was a sudden splintering of timber before it all caved in. Murphy fell backwards from the edge but Cunningham had no time. The boards and clay caught him. His head and shoulders were all that remained above the earth.

He stayed alive while they dug him out but as soon as they released the boards he died. The boards had broken his back.

The most that got through Murphy's shock as he rode with the body in the ambulance to the London Hospital was, 'The police'll be in on this. The assumed names will come out. I might have to have an earlier holiday than I expected.'

The men stood about the site in small silent groups after the ambulance had gone, the different engines idling over, until Barney, the old gangerman, stormed about in his black suit and tie and dirty white shirt, as if he'd suddenly gone epileptic. 'What the fuck are yous all doing? Come on. Get a fukken move on. Do yous think you get fukken paid for standin' about there all day?'

And as the site reluctantly moved back to life a sudden gust of wind lifted an empty cement bag and cartwheeled it across the gravel before wrapping it against the fence of split stakes on Hessell Street.

It was a hot day in Ireland too when the phone rang in the village post office to relay the telegram of the death. The hired girl Mary wrote it down on the official form, closed it in the small green envelope with the black harp and then wondered how to get it delivered. Because of the hot weather everybody else of the post office was in the hayfields two miles away, and she couldn't leave the place unattended to go that far. She decided to cross the road to see if James Sharkey was still in the school. The schoolhouse door was unlocked, and she found the hatted man alone in the classroom. He had stayed behind correcting exam papers.

'What is it, Mary?' he lifted his head from the desk as she tapped on the glass of the classroom door.

'It's Joe Cunningham from Derrada,' she held up the small green envelope. 'He's been killed in an accident in England. And they're all at the hay.'

'Joe Cunningham,' the child's face came to him, a dull average boy, the oldest of the Cunninghams, two of them still at school. He'd been home last summer, boasting and flashing his money in the bars. 'What'll you have, Master? I'm standin' today. We mightn't have been all geniuses but we got on top-pin',' what looked like bits of tinfoil glittering in his jacket.

'I'll take it, Mary. It's just as well I take it. They know me a long time now. I suppose they took the car to the fields?'

'No, they went in the van.'

'I'll take the car then.'

All the doors of the house were open when he got to Cunningham's but there was nobody in. He knew that they must be nearhand, probably at the hay. There is such stillness, stillness of death, he thought, about an empty house with all its doors open on a hot day. A black and white sheepdog left off snapping at flies to rush towards him as he came through the gate into the meadow. It was on the side of the hill above the lake. In the shade, a tin cup floated among some hayseed in a gallon of spring water. Across the lake, just out from a green jet of reeds, a man sat still in a rowboat as if fishing for perch. They were all in the hayfields, the mother and father and four or five children. The field had been raked clean and they were heading off cocks. All work stopped as the hatted man came over the meadow. The father rose from teasing out hay to a boy swinging it into a rope on the tooth of a rake to shout at the dog. They showed obvious discomfort as they waited, probably thinking the teacher had come to complain about some of the children, until they saw the pale green envelope.

'I'm sorry,' the hatted man said as he watched the father read. 'If there's anything I can do you have only to tell me.'

'Joe's been killed in England. The Lord have mercy on his soul,' the father said in dazed quiet, handing the envelope to the mother, all his slow movements heavy with toil.

'Oh my God. My Joe,' the mother broke.

The older children began to cry, but two little girls lifted fistfuls of hay and began to look playfully at one another and the whole stunned hayfield through wisps of hay and to laugh wildly.

'I'll have to go to London. I'll have to take him home,' the father said.

'If there's anything I can do,' the teacher said again.

'Thanks, Master. Shush now,' he said to his wife. 'We'll all go in now. The hay can be tidied up after. Shush now, Bridget. We have to think to do the best by him the few days more he'll be with us,' was the most the teacher remembered as they trooped out of the hayfield towards the house.

'Is there anything—a small drop of something—we can offer you, Master?' they paused at the open door.

'Nothing, thanks, Joe. What I'll do is let you get tidied up and I'll come round for you in about two hours. I'll take you into the town so that you can see to things.'

'Are you sure that won't be putting you to too much trouble, Master?'

'No trouble at all. Why don't you go in now?'

Before he switched on the engine he heard from the open door, 'Thou, Oh Lord, wilt open my lips.' It was the father. And the leaves of the row of poplars along the path from the house were beginning to rattle so loudly in the evening silence that he was glad when the starting engine shut out the sound of leaves.

The father went to London and flew back with the coffin two days later. A long line of cars met the hearse on the Dublin road to follow it to the church. After High Mass the next day young people with white armbands walked behind the hearse until it crossed the bridge, where it gathered speed, and it did not slow until it came in sight of Ardcarne, where they buried him.

Some weeks later the Dance Committee met round the big mahogany table in the front room of the presbytery: the priest, the hatted teacher, the Councillor Doherty, Owen Walsh the sharp-faced postman, and Jimmy McGuire who owned the post office.

'We seem to be nearly all here,' the priest looked round when it had gone well past the time of the meeting.

'We are,' the postman answered quickly. 'Paddy McDermott said he was sorry he couldn't come. It's something to do with sheep.'

'We might as well begin then,' the priest said. 'As we all know why we're here I'll just go over it briefly. Young Cunningham was killed in England. The family insisted on taking the body home. Whether it was wise or foolish it is done now and the only thing we know is that the Cunninghams can't afford to fly a coffin home from England. The talk is that old Joe himself will have to go to England this winter to pay off the expense of the funeral. We all feel, I think, that there's no need for that,' and there was a low murmur of approval.

'So we've more or less decided to hold a dance,' the teacher took up quietly. 'That is unless someone here has a better idea?'

'Have we thought about a collection?' the Councillor Doherty asked because he felt he should ask something.

'The dance more or less covers that as well,' the priest said, and the Councillor nodded comprehendingly. 'Anybody not going will be invited to send subscriptions.'

'I can manage that end of it,' the postman said. 'I can put the word out on my rounds so that it can be done without any fuss.'

'There's no question of getting a big band or anything like that. "Faith, Hope and Charity" will bring in as much and they'll play for a few crates of stout. We'll let people pay whatever they can afford,' the priest said.

'Faith, Hope and Charity' were three old bachelor brothers, the Cryans, who played at local functions. They had been known as 'Faith, Hope and Charity' for so long that nobody now knew how their name began. Faith played the fiddle. Hope beat out the rhythm on the drums. Charity was strapped into an old accordion that was said to have come from America.

'Well, everything seems settled then, so, except the date,' the priest rose when everybody murmured agreement, and unlocked the cabinet. He took out five heavy tumblers and a cut-glass decanter of whiskey. There was already a glass jug of water beside the vase of roses in the centre of the big table.

The dance was held on a lovely clear night in September. A big harvest moon was on the fields. It was almost as clear as day coming to the dance, and the hall was full. Most of the older people came just to show their faces, and by midnight the dance belonged completely to the young. All the Committee left after counting the takings except the postman Owen Walsh and the teacher. They had agreed to stay behind to close the hall. They sat on the table near the door watching the young dance. The teacher had taught nearly all the dancers, and as they paired off to go into the backs of cars or to the fields they were awkward in the tension between their old school relationship with the teacher and their new power as they passed James Sharkey and the postman at the door.

'Now that "Faith, Hope and Charity" are getting into right

old playing form,' the postman nodded humorously toward the empty crates of stout between the three old brothers playing away on the stage, 'they seem to be losing most of their customers.'

'Earlier and earlier they seem to start at it these days. The same old bloody business starting up all over again,' the teacher said.

'Still, I suppose they're happy while they're at it,' the postman smiled, and folded his arms on the table at the door, always feeling himself a bit of an intellectual in these discussions with the hatted teacher, while 'Faith, Hope and Charity' launched into the opening bars of 'A Whistling Gypsy'.

'No, Owen. No. I wouldn't be prepared to go as far as that with you now,' James Sharkey began.

The Stoat

A long-legged student in a turtleneck was following a two-iron he had struck just short of the green when he heard the crying high in the rough grass above the fairway. The clubs rattled as he climbed towards the crying, but it did not cease, its pitch rising. Light of water from the inlet that ran to Ballisadare and was called the Calm Sea blinded him as he climbed out of the coarse tussocks, and he did not see the rabbit at once, where it sat rigidly still on a bare patch of loose sand, screaming; and at the same time he glimpsed the long grey body of the stoat slithering away like a snake into the long grass.

He took a slow step forward but the rabbit still did not move. Its crying ceased, and he noticed the wet slick of blood behind its ear, and then the blood pumping out on the sand. It did not stir when he stooped to pick it up, but never before did he hold such pure terror in his hands, the body trembling in a rigidity of terror as the heart hammered away its blood through the cut in the jugular vein. Holding it up by the hind legs he killed it with one stroke, but when he turned it over he could find no mark other than where the vein had been cut. He took the rabbit down with him, picking his way more cautiously through the long grass than when he had climbed. He left the rabbit beside the clubs while he chipped and holed out, but as he crossed from the green to the tee he saw the stoat cross the fairway behind him. After watching two simple shots fade away into the rough, he knew he had lost his concentration, and decided to finish for the morning. As he made his way back to the cottage his father rented every August in Strandhill, he twice glimpsed the stoat behind him, following the rabbit still, though it was dead.

All night the rabbit must have raced from warren to warren, he thought, the stoat on its trail. Plumper rabbits had crossed the stoat's path but it would not be deflected; it had marked down this one rabbit to kill. No matter how fast the rabbit raced, the stoat was still on its trail, and at last the rabbit sat down in terror and waited for the stoat to slither up and cut the vein behind the ear. He had heard it crying as the stoat was drinking its blood.

His father was reading *The Independent* on the front lawn of the cottage when he got back, facing Knocknarea, his back to the wind that blew from the ocean. A quick look told the son that he was going through the ads for teachers; he always went through the ads for teachers again after he had exhausted the news and death notices, why he would never know, other than from habit or boredom, since he would never leave now the small school where he was principal and the residence that went with it.

'Another colleague who was in Drumcondra the same year as myself has gone to his reward,' he said when he looked up. 'A great full-back poor Weeshie was, God rest him.'

The son made no answer but held up the rabbit.

'Where did you get that?'

'On the links. I heard it crying. And when I went to look there was this weasel. It had cut the jugular vein, and the rabbit was just sitting there. It never moved when I went to pick it up.'

'It must be a stoat. The weasel is extinct in Ireland.'

'A stoat then. I read something about it, but I never came across it before.'

'It's common. You often hear the squealing in scrubs or bushes. No doubt it'll be another specimen for yourself and your uncle to mull over.'

'Well, it's as good as what you find in *The Independent*.'

'What do you intend to do with it?' Other than to rattle the newspaper loudly the father made no response to the counter thrust.

'I thought I'd skin and cook it.'

'Do you think will it be all right?'

'It couldn't be more perfect,' he laughed as he held it up. 'Maybe if I cooked it Miss McCabe might like to have it with us tonight.'

'You better not tell *her* how you came by it,' he looked up in alarm.

'Of course not. Old Luke had rabbits for sale a few days back as well as suspiciously got sea trout and salmon. He said he bought them off fellows with a ferret.'

'Rabbit—the poor man's chicken. What if she doesn't like rabbit?'

'She can say so, and it needn't change anything. There'll be still plenty of time for both of you to have dinner as usual at the Kincora. By the way, what are you going to do for lunch? Are you going to go down to the Bay View?'

'I'd feel like a pint if I went down. If you take a drink too early in this weather it makes the day very cumbersome to get through.'

'There's cheese and bread and a bit of salad. I could make up sandwiches and have coffee.'

'That'd be far better. Good man. Can I give you a hand?'

'No. Stay where you are. I'll bring them out. And what about this rabbit and Miss McCabe. Is it all right with you?'

'I suppose there's no harm in asking her, is there?'

The young student took the rabbit inside. He had no anxieties regarding Miss McCabe and the dinner; she would come even if a cow's head were in question, since by coming to the cottage to dinner she was drawing closer to the dream of her future life, of what she hoped to become.

Miss McCabe's dream was still in the womb of time, he reflected with mock ruefulness, when his father had asked him up to the study the Christmas before. It was not a study in any strict sense, but a small room where he corrected exam papers and kept textbooks and books of his college days, and where he liked to impart decisions in an aura of some solemnity that 'not only affects me, but affects my family as well'. Those occasions that used to arouse fear and foreboding in the growing boy had by this time dwindled to embarrassing and faintly comic charades.

'Would you take it very much to heart if I decided to marry again?' at least that opening had the virtue of surprise.

'Of course not. Why do you ask me?' the young man's face showed his amazement.

'I was afraid you might be affronted by the idea of another woman holding the position your dear mother held,' the voice floated brittlely along on emotion that it could not control. The son hoped the father wouldn't break down and cry, for if he did he was afraid he might idiotically join him. The father started to rotate his thumbs about one another as he waited.

'That's ridiculous. I think you should do exactly what you want to do. It's your life.'

The father looked hurt, as if his life had been brutally severed from the other life by the son's words.

'For years I've been faithful to your mother's memory,' he began painfully. 'Now you're a man. Soon you'll be a fully qualified doctor, while I'll have to eke out my days between this empty house and the school. At my age you don't expect much from marriage, but at least I'd have companionship.'

'There was no need to ask me. In fact, I think it's a good idea.'

'You have no objections then?'

'None. As I said, I think it's a good idea.'

'I'm glad you approve. I wouldn't have gone ahead if you'd any objections.'

The son was curious if there was already some woman in mind, but did not ask. When later that day his father showed him the ad he had written he was grateful for the dismay which cancelled laughter.

Teacher fifty-two. Widower. Seeks companionship. View marriage.

'What do you think of it?'

'I think it's fine. It couldn't be better.'

'I'll send it off then so.'

Neither had any idea that so much unfulfilled longing for the woe that is marriage wandered around in the world till the replies began to pour in. Nurses, housekeepers, secretaries, childless widows and widows with small children, house owners, car owners, pensioners, teachers, civil servants, a policewoman, and a woman who had left at twenty years to work at Fords of Dagenham who wanted to come home to marry. The postman enquired slyly if the school was seeking a new assistant, and the woman who ran the post office said in a faraway voice that if we were looking for a housekeeper she had a relative who might be interested.

'I hope they don't steam the damn letters. This country is on fire with curiosity,' the father complained.

The son saw much of him that spring term, as he met many of the women in Dublin, though he had to go to Cork and Limerick and Tullamore as well. In hotel lounges he met them, hiding behind a copy of the *Roscommon Herald*, which was how they were able to identify him.

'You've never in your life seen such a collection of wrecks and battleaxes as I've had to see in the last few months,' he said, a cold night in late March after he had met the lady from Dagenham in the Ormond. 'You'd need to get a government grant to do them up before you could think of taking some of them on.'

'Do you mean in appearance or as people?'

'All ways,' he said despairingly.

Because of these interviews the son was able to spend all that Easter with his uncle, a surgeon in a county town, who had encouraged him against his father in his choice of medicine, the father wishing to see him in a bank. After dinner, on the first night, the uncle suggested a long walk, 'It's one of those clear frosty nights. We can circle and come back through the town. It's about four miles.'

'That's fine with me.'

A car passed on the road as they set out. The headlamps lit the white railing and fleshly boles of the beech avenue down to the ragged thorns of the road below. They did not start to stride out properly till they reached the road. The three-quarter moon and the stars gave light enough for them to see their breaths in the frosty night.

'My father's going to get married, it seems,' he confided, in the ring of the footsteps.

'You're joking,' his uncle paused.

'I'm not. He's had an ad this long while in the papers.'

'An ad. You're surely joking.'

'I'm not. I'm in deadly earnest.'

'An ad,' suddenly the uncle became convulsed with laughter, and was hardly able to get the next words out, 'And did he get . . . replies?'

'Bundles. He's been interviewing them.'

'And have you seen any of the . . . applicants,' he had to pause again on the road.

'No, but he said you'd need a government grant to do some of them that he's seen up before you could think of marrying them.'

'A government grant . . . stop it. This is high farce. The man must finally have gone off his rocker.'

'Apparently he's just found someone. A schoolteacher in her forties. She's no beauty, but a shining light compared with the wrecks and battleaxes he's been interviewing.'

'Have you seen this person?'

'Not yet. I'm supposed to see her next week.'

'My god, if you hang round long enough you see everything,'

he combed his fingers through his long greying hair as he walked. 'At least, if he does get married, it'll get him off your back.'

'You don't like my father much?'

'He's a decent enough fellow but I find him dull. Probably not nearly as dull as he finds me.'

They had circled the town. Lighted poles appeared in the thorn hedges, and then a paved sidewalk.

'We might as well have a drink in the Grand Central,' the uncle said as they came into the town. 'The trouble with being a bigwig in a small town is that there's either the Grand Central or nowhere,' and though he nodded to some people sitting in armchairs as they passed through the lounge, he headed straight for a corner of the bar. 'We'll stand. That way we can't be so easily cornered. You know, if your father does succeed in getting himself hitched, you'll be able to spend much more time here. I'd like that.'

He'd like that too. With his uncle everything seemed open: 'Life seems to have no purpose other than to reproduce itself. Life comes out of matter and goes back into matter. We inherit it and pass it on. We might as well take as decent a care of it as we can. You cannot go against love and not be in error.' Nothing was closed. This freedom was gaiety, even though it seemed that it caused him to seem mostly lonely.

'I feel guilty about it but the truth is that my father bores me. I fear and hate the unconscious.'

A few Saturdays later he was to meet Miss McCabe in Dublin. Both his father and she were desperately nervous. It made him feel that he was the parent and they the children anxious for his approval. Miss McCabe wore pale tweeds and serviceable brown shoes. She was somewhere in her forties, rather frail, and excitable. He liked her, but he would have encouraged his father to marry her whether he did or not, as he was anxious for the whole play to be over.

'Well, what was your impression?' his father asked him afterwards. That she was so desperately nervous that she spilled both coffee and a small bowl of cream at the luncheon, that she was anxious for approval to such a point that no person should or ought to be from another . . . these he did not say. Who was he to give or to withhold approval from one who had been wandering round in the world long before he.

'I think Miss McCabe is a fine person,' he said.

'You have . . . no objections then?'

'Of course not.'

'I'm glad,' he said and started to explain their plans.

She would come with them to Strandhill this summer, and stay in one of the hotels close to the usual cottage they took for August. If all went well they would become engaged before they went back to the schools at the end of the holidays.

They had been at Strandhill a week now, the boy golfing or studying, the father spending much of his time with Miss McCabe. Sometimes the son would see them arm in arm on the promenade from the tees close to the shore. The sight disturbed him, as if their defence was too brittle against the only end of life, and made it too disturbingly obvious, and he would try to shut it out with the golf ball.

'Will you be seeing Miss McCabe?' the boy asked as he put the coffee and sandwiches on the table.

'I might drop into the hotel. She's going to the salt baths.'

There was a hot salt bath close to where the old cannon pointed out on the ocean, asbestos covered, the yellow funnel of a ship for chimney from which plumes of steam puffed. She went every afternoon for the hot baths and a massage. She had rheumatism.

'And you? What do you intend? Are you studying?'

'No, I'll get in a round, and come back early to cook that rabbit. But ask Miss McCabe. It's just a folly on my part to want to cook it, and I don't mind at all if you'd both prefer to eat as usual at the Kincora.'

They left the cottage together after lunch, the father with a walking stick, the son with the golf clubs, and parted at the lane that led to the clubhouse.

As he went round the course he climbed in that instinct that draws people to places that have witnessed murder or violence to where he had heard the crying that morning, but the blood had dried from the sand, and the place was uncannily still, the coarse tussocks rustling in the sea wind, the strand covered with the full tide, and a white sailing boat tacking up the inlet from Ballisadare to the mouth of the ocean.

He skinned and dressed the rabbit that evening, clinically teasing out the dried blood where the vein had been cut, and Miss McCabe came at eight. The father was plainly uneasy until she exclaimed that the rabbit was delicious.

'I never knew rabbit could be so good,' he added. 'I suppose it's just prejudice again. It was always known as the poor man's chicken.'

'We must praise the cook too. As well as a future doctor we have also a good cook on our hands,' Miss McCabe was so much in her element that she was careless. 'It's much nicer to eat here than at the Kincora. Luke seems to have very good trout as well. Some of them look as fat as butter. You must allow me to cook them for dinner some evening soon. It's crazy not to have fish when at the ocean.'

'Miss McCabe likes you enormously,' the father sang after he had returned from leaving her back to the hotel. 'She has savings, and she says you'll be welcome to them if you ever need money for post-graduate work or anything like that.'

'That won't be necessary. My uncle said I can have as much as I need on loan for those purposes,' the son said cuttingly, and the reference to the uncle annoyed the father as much as Miss McCabe's offer had the son. Irrationally, he felt soiled by meal and rabbit and whole evening, as if he had taken part in some buffoonery against the day, against any sense of dignity, and he was determining how to avoid the trout dinner and anything more got to do with them.

As it turned out there was no need for avoidance. A uniformed bellhop came from the hotel the next evening to tell that Miss McCabe had suffered a heart attack in the salt baths that afternoon. The doctor had seen her and she was resting in her hotel room. She wished to see the father.

'Will you come?' the father asked.

'It's you she wants to see.'

When he got back from the hotel he was incredibly agitated. He could not sit still.

'She's all right,' he said. 'She just had a mild heart attack in the hot baths, but she still thinks we'll get engaged at the end of the month.'

'But I thought that was the general idea.'

'It was. If everything went well. Who wants to marry a woman who can pop off at any minute?'

It sometimes happened, even in the act, the son had heard, but he said nothing.

'Isn't it enough to have buried one woman?' the father shouted.

'Did you tell her?'

'I tried. I wasn't able. All she thinks of is our future. Her head is full of plans.'

'What are you going to do?'

'Clear out,' he said, to the son's dismay.

'You can't do that.'

'It's the only way to do it. I'll write to her.'

'What . . . if she doesn't take it?'

'There's nothing I can do about that.'

As if all the irons were being suddenly all truly struck and were flowing from all directions to the heart of the green, he saw with terrifying clarity that it was the stoat the father had glimpsed in Miss McCabe's hotel room, and he was running.

'What'll you do about the cottage? It's rented till the end of the month.'

'It doesn't matter about the cottage. The rent is paid.'

"Where'll you go to?'

'Home, of course. Aren't you coming?' he asked as if he assumed it was foregone.

'No,' he saw his chance, 'I'll stay.'

'What if Miss McCabe sees you?' the father asked in alarm.

'There's nothing I can do for her or she for me.'

He was not staying by the sea either. Tomorrow he would leave for his uncle's. They were all running.

'What if she asks about me?'

'Naturally, I'll try to avoid her, but if I meet her I'll say I don't know. That it's not my affair. How soon are you going?'

'As soon as I get the stuff into the boot of the car.'

'I'll give you a hand so.'

'Are you sure you won't change your mind?'

'No. I'll stay.'

'Write then.'

'I'll write.'

Already he could hear his uncle's mordant voice. 'You have to take a test to drive a bloody old car around. But any pair of imbeciles of age can go and take a marriage licence out and set about bringing a child up in the world, which is a much more complicated activity than driving an old car around!' There would be good talk for several days, and there was the story of the stoat and the rabbit.

All night the rabbit must have raced from warren to warren, the stoat on its trail. Plumper rabbits had crossed the stoat's path but it would not be deflected; it had marked down this one rabbit to kill. No matter how fast the rabbit raced, the stoat was still on its trail, and at last the rabbit sat down in terror and waited for the stoat to slither up and cut the vein behind the ear. He had heard it crying as the stoat was drinking its blood.

Doorways

There are times when we see the small events we look forward to—a visit, a wedding, a new day—as having no existence but in the expectation. They are to be, they will happen, and before they do they almost are not: minute replicas of the expectation that we call the rest of our life.

I used to panic when I saw life that way, it brought the blind and overmastering desire to escape, and the religious life had seemed for long the one way out: to resign this life, to take on the habit of unchanging death-like days, the sweet passion; and when death came it could hold no terror, one had already died in life.

I no longer panic when I see that way: nature, having started to lose interest in me, is now content to let me drift away, and no longer jabs me so sharply that I must lose myself in life before it is too late.

And I have found Barnaby and Bartleby. They are all day and every day in the doorways of Abbey Street. I call them Barnaby and Bartleby but I do not know their names. They must have some shelter to go to, for they disappear from the doorways about eight in winter, an hour later in the summer. I have never seen them leave. They seem to be there one moment and gone the next. I have never watched them go. I feel it would be an intrusion to draw too close at that time and that they mightn't leave if watched. The early morning is the one time they are busy, searching the bins with total concentration before the garbage trucks come by. They never search the same bin together or stand in the same doorway. Only in freezing weather

71

do they come close, just inside the door of the Public Lavatory, and even there they keep the red coinslot weighing machine between them, their backs to the wall, above their heads the black arrow pointing to the urinal stalls within.

They seem to change doorways every two hours or so and always to the same doorway at the same time. I thought at first they might be following the sun but then noticed they still changed whether the sun was in or out. They wear long overcoats, tightly belted, with pleats at the back, that had been in fashion about fifteen years before. Often I want to ask them why have they picked on this way to get through life, but outside the certainty of not being answered I soon see it as an idle question and turn away. They never answer strangers who ask about the times of the buses out of Abbey Street. They have their different ways, too, of not answering. Bartleby, the younger and smaller, just moves his boots and averts his face sideways and down; but Barnaby stares steadily over his steel-rimmed spectacles into his interlocutor's eyes. Otherwise, they seem to take a calm and level interest in everything that goes on outside their doorway. They must be completely law abiding, for the police hardly glance at them as they pass on patrol.

ii

It was in the first winter that I began to be fascinated with Barnaby and Bartleby that I met Kate O'Mara. We met at Nora Moran's.

Nora Moran was a painter who gave parties round people she hoped would buy her paintings or get her grants from foundations or advance her career or self-esteem; in some way they were all intertwined. We used to make fun of Nora: 'I ran into Nora Moran today. She's in a bad way. She's down to her last three houses,' after listening to her money worries in some coffee shop off the Green for numbing hours as the coffee went cold and the cups were taken away, for in our eyes she was a rich and successful woman; but we still went to her parties, knowing we were being used as butcher's grass or chopped-down rhododendron branches to cover up the dusty margins of the processional ways in June. We went out of respect for Nora's early work and, less honourably, because it took a greater energy to stay away than go once Nora had made up her mind that we should go. As young women were not Nora's idea of either butcher's grass or rhododendrons, it was with surprise that I found myself facing a tall and lovely young woman at a party of Nora's, close to Christmas.

'Hi,' she said at once. 'My name is Kate O'Mara, I'm American.'

'How do you happen to be here at Nora's?' I couldn't help asking as soon as the courtesies were over.

'I used to work on this magazine in the States,' she said gaily. 'The editor is a friend of Nora's. We did a big thing on her last year. And when I was coming to Dublin everybody said I must go and see her.'

'You're here on holiday?'

'No,' she said, laughing. 'I guess you won't believe it. I'll be here for a year or more. I came here to write.'

There are so many voices here already, and so little room. Who will hear all the voices, I thought, but as I saw Nora Moran moving towards us I asked quickly, 'Will you let me take you out to dinner some evening?'

'Sure,' she answered uncertainly, surprised.

'If you have a phone I'll ring you then. I see Nora is pushing our way.'

I had just time to write down the telephone number and conceal the paper when I heard Nora's voice, 'Well, what are you two getting up to here?' and when the social laughter ceased, 'Kate was telling me about this profile of you that appeared in America last year.'

There was no need to say more. Nora was launched warmly on her favourite subject.

iii

'Why were you so anxious to keep from Nora that we were going out to dinner?' were almost the first words she asked the following Saturday when we were seated in a corner of the restaurant.

'She'd want to come.'

'I don't believe it.'

'You will. It's control,' and then I asked, looking at her ring-less fingers, 'Were you ever married?'

'No. Why do you ask?' The soup spoon paused at her lips in surprise.

'No why. It's probably just a stupid generalization. We think of Americans here as much married.'

'My mother would have a fit if she heard that. We're Catholics from way back. Nuns and priests galore. "No one was ever divorced in *my* family," my mother is fond of boasting.'

'Has that anything to do with your coming here to try to write?'

'In a way. The whole family is rotten with nostalgia about Ireland, so I said I'd come and see into it once and for all myself. And it *was* easier to come here. If I said I was going to wicked Paris, there'd be an uproar, but old Dublin is a nice, clean, little old place. So here I am.'

'And you look quite lovely,' I said sincerely, and the rest of the meal went as easily.

'Why don't we split this? This place isn't cheap,' she said when the bill came.

'No. This is mine. Another time you can take me if you wish,' and when we were outside I said, 'It's only a few streets. I'll walk you home.'

Below the granite steps that led to the Georgian doorway where she had rooms I leaned to kiss her. She did not withdraw, but turned her cheek, making clear it was no more than a courtesy at the end of the evening.

'Would you like to come out some other evening?' I asked, awkwardly in the rebuff that was not quite a rebuff.

'Sure,' she said openly. 'The next time I must take you. When?'

'Say, next Saturday.'

She thought for a moment and said, 'Next Saturday's fine. And thanks for the evening,' and waved as she took the key out of her purse.

Aimlessly, like old people grateful for mere human presence, we went out together that winter. Only once did I challenge the sexual restraints she put on the relationship.

'Is there someone that you're sexually involved with?' I asked in concealed frustration one evening.

'Yes.'

'Is it someone in Dublin?' I loathed asking but could not hold back.

She simply named a man I knew, in public relations, whom she had met at Nora Moran's.

'He has this dream of an Irish Ireland, free of outside influences, and he's fiercely anti-American. I get abused all the time for being American,' she explained.

'Do you want to marry him?'

'No,' she laughed. 'I'm not quite that crazy. It just couldn't happen anyhow.'

'But you sleep with him?' I felt as if I was probing my own flesh with a sharp instrument but I could not stop.

'Yes, but it's a bad business. He always leaves as soon as it's over. Whenever we meet it's he who does all the talking and we only meet whenever he wants, not when I want, and yet I keep missing him.'

'I'm sorry,' I said in the face of her honesty.

'No. It's a relief to talk about these things sometimes.'

Even so, she must have suspected my desire or jealousy, and feared it, for whenever after I would ask about her life outside our meetings she would avoid a direct answer or deliberately make her life sound more humdrum and dull than it could be, and she always wore her plainest clothes.

iv

It was with a smile of poor irony that I noticed the light of competition in Nora Moran's eyes when next we met.

'We hardly ever see you now,' were her first words, 'but I hear you and Kate see a great deal of one another. She's a very attractive girl.'

'We see each other very little. But people exaggerate. Several times I was going to call you, but then I thought you'd be too busy.'

'Well, let's drop everything today. I've been intending to go down to the farm for long. Let's both go today.'

'That's fine with me.'

There was a mist that promised to break into a fine day as we drove out of the city. Nora had a large heavy car, with warm mahogany panelling; and she drove very fast, and badly, continually taking her eyes off the road to search my face for responses.

'Do you see that beech tree over there, Nora?' I resorted to saying when we got out into the country. 'There's something about its trunk that reminds me of some of the recurring shapes in your work,' leaning cravenly towards the windscreen to narrow her angle when she would look back; and it was with real relief I sank back when the car lurched into the long gravelled avenue that led to the house.

'I lose money on it all the time,' she said as we looked over the rich acres, 'but it's the last thing I'd ever sell. My father built up this place from nothing. I like to think he'd approve of everything I've done since he died if he were to come back.'

'Still, with the way money is it's a solid investment.'

'He was fond of saying that. "Never be fool enough to keep your money in cash." You'd have loved my father,' she said,

76

warming. 'He was that sort of a man if he were to take a fork to his soup at a dinner table all the others would take up their forks too. "You have us all brainwashed, Mr Moran," old Michael, the gardener, used to say to him. He was the only one who dared say it, he was with us so long.'

After meeting the herdsmen, and the two farmhands, we opened the big white house, and went through it room by room. Nora's paintings hung on the walls alongside paintings her father had purchased, many of them valuable. I managed to leave most of the discussion to Nora by saying that I had no faith in my judgement, not having been brought up with pictures, but that I liked everything in the house. Late in the evening I made a log fire in the dining room while Nora made cheese and tomato sandwiches. We had sandwiches, with a half-bottle of red wine Nora brought from the cellar, at a corner of the long table.

'Do you ever miss not being married, Nora?' I asked so as not to appear too passive, though it did not matter.

'No. My life is too full for me to be ever married, but sometimes I wish I had someone, a young man making his way in the world, an academic, or young artist perhaps. I'd set him up close to me. We'd make no demands on one another. All I'd ask is that between certain hours I could come to him if I was tired,' and she looked at me so steadily that I began to feel uneasy, and changed the subject to her paintings.

Afterwards, I took nothing in of the long river of words, like the body unable to absorb excess of vitamins; and I only took care to make the barest responses. By the time we left they were not even necessary. I was glad of the dark in the car as we drove back to the city, both of us keeping our eyes fixed on the empty floodlit roads. The black hands of an orange clockface on a steeple were fixed at twelve-ten as we reached the outskirts of the city.

'Do you mind if I drop round to mother before leaving you off?' she said. 'I never feel easy without saying goodnight to mother. She may have been looking for me on the phone all day.'

'I don't mind at all.'

'It'll be little more than a minute out of our way.'

We crossed a cattle grid into the courtyard of a luxury block of flats, and Nora drove round to the side.

Suddenly, without switching the engine off, she started to blow the horn. She blew until a fragile old woman in a night-dress appeared in the groundfloor window. 'Goodnight, mother,' Nora rolled down the window, and waved, and blew the horn again. The old mother waved feebly back, without seeming certain of what she was waving at, as Nora reversed the car, and blew a last time.

'It costs a fortune to keep mother in that place, but she's never satisfied. She never rings up but that she has some com-plaint or other. My father was too proud to admit it, but his marriage was the one real failure in his life. She was never in his style.'

'It'll be all right if you let me out here, Nora. I'd be glad of the few minutes' walk. And thanks for the lovely day.'

We grimaced and waved goodnight to one another like any special pair of monkeys. I was numbed by the day, I was prob-ably numbed anyhow, and I hadn't even resentment of my own passivity; but certainly Barnaby and Bartleby were far closer to my style than any of this day had been.

And as soon as I thought of them in their doorways, the sound of my own footsteps in the empty silence of a sleeping city seemed to take on a kind of healing.

v

I now took, if anything, a keener interest in Barnaby and Bartle-by, since my aimless ambulations with Kate O'Mara, the poor day with Nora Moran, seemed to echo loosely their far stricter observances in the doorways. Barnaby's sallow face behind the steel rims did not change as the winter gave way to a hot early summer, but Bartleby positively bloomed in the doorways, and even in his rigidly belted overcoat looked as tanned as if he had just come from the seaside.

Later, Barnaby did start to sport a plastic yellow cap, such as girl bicyclists wear in rain, and to make sudden gestures. I put it down to the irritation of the heat, and it was enough to suggest that I go on holiday. Instead of going abroad I had a sudden desire to go to the sea that I had gone to as a child. I wrote to Jimmy McDermott in Sligo. We had grown up together, gone to our first dances there, taken girls we had met at the dances in harmless summers to Dollymount and Howth; and before the time came for us to drift naturally apart he was transferred to Sligo. I wrote to him to ask if he could find me a cheap room in Sligo for the summer and he wrote back that there was room in his own place and that he would be glad if I came. About the same time Kate O'Mara told me that her affair had ended.

'What happened?'

'He got married. There were even pictures in the papers with confetti and buttonhole carnations,' she said with self-mocking bitterness. 'He'd even the gall to come round and tell me about it, saying sanctimoniously how things would never have worked out between us anyhow. Practically asked my blessing.'

'And what did you do?'

'I told him to get lost, to go to hell.'

'Good girl,' I said. 'But how do you feel now?'

'My vanity took a hammering. I guess I'm not used to that. It couldn't come to anything anyhow.'

'You should have gone out with me instead and maybe we'd be married now.'

'Thanks,' she laughed, 'but that could never be.'

I told her I was going on holiday for the summer, to Sligo. 'Maybe if I find it all right you might like to come down later,' I said.

'I doubt it. I have to try to work. I've hardly done any work in the last month.'

'I'll write you. Maybe you may want to change your mind.'

I thought her face very pale and strained as she waved me goodbye.

vi

Jimmy met me at Sligo Station. He had put on weight and one could see the light through his thinning hair, but the way the porters and the drivers playing cards at the taxi rank hailed him he was as popular here as he had been everywhere. Soon, walking with him and remembering the part of our lives that had been passed together, it was like walking in a continuance of days rather than in the broken worlds of ourselves. It was an illusion but it was comfortable. And isn't there a whole school of thought that says all of life is an illusion. . . .

'I hope getting the digs didn't put you to a great deal of trouble,' I said.

'No. The old birds were pleased as punch. Ordinarily it's full, but this time they've always rooms because of people gone on holidays.'

The old birds were two sisters in their fifties, who owned the big stone house down by the harbour where Jimmy had digs and where I had come on holiday. A brother who was a Monsignor in California had bought it for them and I had never seen before walls so completely laden with cribs and religious pictures. There was the usual smell of digs, of cooking and feet and sweat, the sharp scent of HP sauce, as much suggested by the brown bottle on every lino-covered table as by any actual smell.

'They're religious mad but they're good sorts and they won't bother you. They have to cook for more than thirty,' Jimmy said after he had introduced me and showed me to my room, mockingly sprinkling holy water from a font between the feet of a large statue of the Virgin as he left. There were at least thirty men at tea that evening. Out of the aggressive bantering and horseplay as they ate, fear and insecurity and hatred of one another came to me like a familiar face.

'It's the usual,' Jimmy said when I mentioned it to him afterwards as we walked to the pub to talk. He was excited and greedy for news of the city. He even asked about Barnaby and Bartleby, 'The gents of Abbey Street'.

'Why do you remember them?'

'I don't know. I never paid them any attention when I was there. It's only since I came here that I started to think about them.'

'But why?'

'I suppose,' he said slowly, 'they highlight what we're all at.'

'Do you miss the city then?'

'I don't know. I suppose. In a way my life ended when I left it. When I was there it still seemed to have possibilities, but now I know it's all fixed.'

'And that girl—was it Mary Jo?' I named a dark, swarthy girl, extraordinarily attractive rather than goodlooking.

'The Crystal, National, Metropole, Clerys', he repeated the names of the ballrooms. 'She went to England.'

'Why didn't you keep her?'

'Maybe it wasn't possible. There seemed so much time then that there was no hurry. I went to London to try to see her but she was working at Littlewoods and had shacked up with a married Englishman.' I could tell that he had suffered and changed. 'Do you have anyone here?'

'Yes. There was so much choice in Dublin. But here, if you get anything, you have to hold on to it as if it was your life, there are so few women here,' he sounded as if he was already apologizing for her. She was a dark pretty girl but she never spoke a word when we met. I noticed that only when alone with Jimmy did she grow animated.

'And you, have you anybody?' he asked.

81

'No. There's an American girl, but there's nothing sexual between us. I'm coming to the age when you have to start thinking about throwing your hat at it. We're just friends,' and when
I saw that he didn't believe me I added, 'There's a slight chance
she may still come down.'

The Blue Anchor was filling. All of the men nodded to Jimmy
and many of them joined us with their pints. When an old
fisherman came, Jack Kelly, place was made for him in the
centre of the party beside Jimmy. It turned out that they were
all members of the newly formed Pint Drinkers' Association.
Jack Kelly was the President and Jimmy was both Secretary and
Treasurer. The publicans of the town had got together and fixed
a minimum price for the pint, a few pence higher than what
had been charged previously. The Pint Drinkers' Association
had been formed to fight this rise. They canvassed bars and
pledged that the Pint Drinkers would drink only at those bars
that kept to the old price. There cannot have been great soli-
darity among the publicans, for already six, including the Blue
Anchor, which had become the Association's headquarters, had
agreed to return to the old price. When I paid over the fee
Jimmy wrote my name down in a child's blue exercise book and
Jack Kelly silently witnessed it. Soon afterwards we left the
Blue Anchor and began a round of the bars.

Time went by without being noticed in the days that followed:
watching the boats in the harbour, leaning on the bridge of
Sligo, the white foam churning under the weir, a weed or fish
swaying lazily to the current; newsprint-darkened hands from
the morning's paper on some windowsill or bar stool; the sea
at Rosses and Strandhill. Often in the evenings we played hand-
ball at the harbour alley, and though our hands were swollen
and all our muscles ached, it was as if the years had fallen away,
and we were striking the small rubber inside the nettingwire of
the school, the cabbage stumps in the black clay of the garden
between the alley and orchard. Afterwards we would meet in
the Blue Anchor, from where we could set out on our nightly

round of the bars that had agreed to keep the pint at its old price, and as their number was growing steadily, it made for thirsty work.

'It's catching on like wildfire,' I said to Jimmy as we lurched away from the last bar one evening, voluble with six or seven pints.

'I'll wait and see,' Jimmy said. 'It'll probably be like everything else here. It'll catch on for a while. And then fall away.'

At this time Jimmy began to miss three evenings every week now that the Association, as he put it, was on a firm footing. He took his girl to the cinema or went dancing, and this disturbed Jack Kelly.

'Jimmy's beginning to show the white flag,' he complained. 'He's missing again this evening. Watch my word. The leg-irons will be coming up soon.'

vii

This pleasant wallow might have gone on for weeks except for a card I sent to Kate O'Mara. I wrote that I was happy at the sea, and that if she changed her mind and wished to join me to just write. Instead, she telegrammed that she was coming on the early train the next day. I booked two single rooms in a small hotel at Strandhill and Jimmy and I met her off the train. She was wearing sandals, and had on a sleeveless dress of blue denim, and dark glasses.

'Jimmy's an old friend. I thought we'd all have a glass and some sandwiches,' I said when she seemed puzzled by Jimmy's presence.

'I actually had something on the train. I didn't know.'

'That doesn't matter. You can have a drink,' Jimmy said as we took her bags.

'I'm afraid that I'm not a big drinker, Jimmy,' she laughed nervously.

'What'll you have?' I asked her in a bar down from the station, quiet with three porters discussing the racing page as they finished their lunch hour.

'I'll take a chance,' she grew more easy. 'Can I have an Irish coffee?' but when it came all our attempts at speech were awkward, and as soon as he could Jimmy made a show of examining his watch and rose. 'Some of the population has to work,' he grinned ruefully.

'I'll come in tomorrow or the next day,' I said.

'I'll keep any letters for you then,' he said.

'How were you in Dublin?' I asked when we were alone.

'His marriage hit me worse than I thought. I could do nothing but mope or cry,' at once she took up the story of her broken affair.

She hadn't been able to work or read and she began to go to the Green, sitting behind dark glasses in one of the canvas deck-chairs placed in a half-circle round the fountain in hot weather; and she just sat there watching the people pass, or remembering her life in New York, and was gradually growing calm when one day Nora Moran found her and took her down the country. The day seemed to have turned out an exact replica of the day I had spent.

'And the workmen were so servile with her,' Kate complained in a shocked voice.

'They don't mind that. That's their way,' I said.

'But American workmen would never be like that.'

'That's different. They've a different way over there.'

'Listen, won't we miss the bus?' an edge had crept into the talk.

'You don't want to listen to me about Nora?'

'I do, but you should know that Nora needs a fresh person every day in the same way other people need a bottle of whiskey.'

'If she wasn't around she was on the phone. A few nights ago, as she was going on about herself on the phone, you'd think I had no life at all, and I just couldn't help it and began to cry. I must have cried for ten minutes, and when I picked up the phone again, there was Nora still in full song. She hadn't even noticed that I hadn't been listening.'

'Still, you don't have to worry now,' I gripped her shoulders. 'You're here now. And it is very beautiful.'

'I can't tell you how happy I am to be here,' she said as we went to the bus. The bus dropped us at the church across from the hotel. A large taciturn man, Costello, had us sign our names in the register and then showed us to our rooms on separate floors.

viii

The eight o'clock bells woke me the next morning, it was a Sunday; and we came downstairs almost together. She had on a black lace scarf and leather gloves and a missal with a simple gold cross.

'Are you going to Mass before having breakfast?' I asked.

'Yes,' she laughed a light girlish laugh.

'I'll come too,' I said, and since she was looking at me in surprise I added, 'It makes a good impression round here,' as we walked across and joined other worshippers on the white gravel between the rows of escallonia that led to the church door. I remembered her saying once, 'I'm a bad Catholic but I am one because if I wasn't I couldn't bear all the thinking I'd have to do'; and for me, as I knelt by her side in the church or stood or sat, it was more like wandering in endless corridors of lost mornings than being present in this actual church and day, always in the same barn with wings to the left and right of the altar and the cypress and evergreen still in the windows.

'We'll have you reconverted soon,' she said playfully as she sprinkled holy water in my direction as we left by the porch door.

'No, but I wish I could be. But once you've lost it you can't go back. If I went back now I'd know I was going back as a

85

Catholic, and the whole point of it is not being able to imagine being anything else.'

'In that sense I'm hardly one either.'

'I think we should have breakfast,' I hurried her quickly past the people shaking hands at the gate to the hotel.

Sunday was suddenly again for me what it had been once. The first bell for Second Mass was more than an hour away, and we had already done our duty. We had changed out of our stiff Sunday suits and the shoes we had to be careful of, and the day was still before us, for football or pitch-and-toss or the river; and the whole day stretched before us in such a long, amazing prospect of pleasure and excitement that we were almost loath to begin it.

With the same recovery of amazement I watched Kate's beauty against the power of the ocean as we walked afterwards on the shore, traced the fading initials on the wood of the cannon pointed out to sea, watched the early morning golfers strike off for the clubhouse, and saw the children come out with their buckets and beach balls, watched by their parents from the edge of the rocks.

'We can have all this and more,' began to beat like a madness in my blood.

ix

As it was a hot Sunday, I knew that relatives or people I had known would come to the sea, for the 'ozone', as they used to say, and if I hung about the hotels or front I was bound to meet them.

'I think I'll steer clear of the beaten track for the next five or six hours,' I said to her at lunch, and explained why.

'What do you care? Are you too shy?' she asked sharply.

'It'd be stupid to be shy at my age. It'd be just a burden to make conversation, they and I are now different people and yet still the same. And I just don't want to have to act out the farce.'

When she was silent I said, 'You don't have to come if you don't want to.'

'Where'll you go?'

'I'll take a book or something over to that old roofless church you can barely see in the far distance.'

'I guess I'll come—that's if you have no objection,' she said, and there was already tension.

'I'll only be glad.'

As we walked I pointed to the stream of cars going slowly down to the sea. The roofless church was two miles from the hotel. At first, close to the hotels, we had come across some half-circles of tents in the hollows, then old single tents, and soon there was nothing but the rough sea grass and sand and rabbit warrens. Some small birds flew out of the ivy rooted in the old walls of the church, and we sat among the faceless stones, close to a big clump of sea thistle. Far away the beach was crowded with small dark figures within the coastguard flags.

'In America,' she said, looking at the lighthouse, 'they have a bell to warn ships. On a wet misty evening it's eerie to hear it toll, like lost is the wanderer.'

'It must be,' I repeated. I felt I should say something about it and there was nothing I could say.

'It is—in a sad way,' and we began to read, but the tension between us increased rather than lessened, whether from me or from her or from us both. I saw the white tinsel of the sea thistle, the old church, the slopes of Knocknarea, the endless pounding of the ocean mingled with bird and distant child cries, the sun hot on the old stones, the very day in its suspension, and thought if there was not this tension between us, if only we could touch or kiss we could have all this and more, the whole day and sea and sky and far beyond.

'This country depresses me so much it makes me mad,' she said suddenly.

'Why?' I looked slowly up.

'Everybody comes to the beach and just sits around. In America they'd be doing handstands, playing volleyball, riding the surf. Forgive me for saying that, but I had to say something.'

'I don't mind at all.'

'That's part of the trouble. You should mind.'

'I don't mind.' I thought that if we were Barnaby and Bartleby we could hardly be further apart.

'Kate,' I said suddenly, 'why can't you sleep with me?'

'I couldn't,' she shook her head and smiled.

'You're free now. We could have so much more together. And if nothing came of it we have very little to lose anyway.'

'No. I don't think of you that way. I couldn't.'

'Why not?'

'No. I'm sorry,' she shook her head. 'I couldn't think of us that way. I think we have far more just because we haven't.'

I thought bitterly of what she said—like Nora Moran's workmen I had been brought up a different way, that was all— but asked, 'You mean you can't think of us as ever being married?'

'I'm very fond of you but I could never think of us in that way. I think we're far too alike for that.'

'Still, I had to ask you,' I conceded I had lost. She did not want me that way as some people cannot eat shell fish or certain meats. There was once a robin who sang against the church bells striking midnight, thinking that the yellow street lamps in the road below were tokens of the day.

Hours later, in the tiredness of the evening, spaces now on the hill between the cars leaving the beach for the day, she said gently, 'I hope it'll make no difference between us.'

'It won't.'

'I think we can have far more as we are,' she said, 'that what's between us is only beginning.'

'Maybe,' I echoed. 'It's the way it seems it must be.'

X

The next day was wet, a mist that closed in from the sea so that the church was barely visible from the hotel, but though the rain was soft as a caress on the face it wet one through. I played billiards all that morning in a bar down on the front, and then rang Jimmy. I arranged to meet him in Sligo.

'I'm going to Sligo, to pick up letters this evening. Would you like to come?' I asked her over lunch.

'Why?'

'Jimmy and his girl are going to the cinema, and he asked if we'd like to go with them and have a drink afterwards.'

'Like two happy couples,' she said derisively.

'Well, you don't have to come,' I said, and we began to talk about Nora Moran. The more we talked the more I felt how real and honest was Nora's brutal egotism set against our pale lives here by the sea.

'If Nora has ears to hear they must be burning now,' she laughed when we had ended.

'Still, in spite of it, she has something,' I was forced to say.

We went to our rooms to read. Outside the window the road shone black with rain, and through the mist it was as if fine threads of rain were being teased slowly down. We did not meet till the flat gong that hung in the hallway rang for tea.

'You haven't changed your mind?' I asked cautiously.

'Listen,' she said. 'I want you to do something for me. I want you not to go to Sligo.'

'But I can't not go. I promised Jimmy.'

'You can call him up.'

'There's no phone in the digs and he's left work by now.'

She was eating so slowly that I began to fear I would miss the bus if I waited for her.

'I'm sorry. I have to go,' I said as I rose.

'Do you have to go so soon?'

'The bus'll be outside in five minutes or so.'

To my puzzlement she laid her knife and fork side by side on the plate, rose, took her raincoat from the bentwood stand in the hall, and came out with me into the rain. In uncomfortable silence we watched the bus pass down, waited for it to turn at the cannon and come back, the waves crashing incessantly on the shore beyond the soft, endlessly drifting veils of rain.

'Are you sure you won't change your mind and come?' I asked as I heard the bus.

'No,' she shook her head, and as the veiled yellow sidelights showed in the rain she suddenly tugged my sleeve and said earnestly, 'I want you to do this for me. I want you not to get on the bus.'

'Is there any good reason?' I demanded. Only a beloved could ask so much, so capriciously. Did she want all this as well as the voices, without any of the burden of love or work?

'Just that I want you not to go.'

'I can't not go,' I said, 'but what I'll do is get the next bus back. I'll be back within an hour. Maybe we'll go out for a drink then,' and pressing her arm climbed on the bus. As soon as I paid the conductor I looked back, but already the bus had changed gear to climb the hill and I could not see through the rain and misted windows whether she was still standing there or had gone back into the hotel, and I stirred uneasily in the sense that I had left some hurt behind. Yet what she had demanded had been unreasonable, but far more insistently than reason or the grinding of the bus came, 'If you had loved her you would have stayed'; but all life turns away from its own eventual hopelessness, leaving insomnia and its night to lovers and the dying.

I had come far in time since first I travelled on this bus. Surprised then by the conductor's outstretched hand, I had reached up and shaken it. The whole bus had rocked with laughter and one man cheered. 'It's the fare now I'd be looking for,' and though he had smiled the conductor had been as embarrassed and confused as I.

As much through the light of years as through this wet evening the bus seemed to move. It was an August evening. We were going home at the end of another summer holiday. When the bus stopped at the Central, Michael Henry got on. His clothes hung about him, and the only sign of his old jauntiness was the green teal's feather in the felt hat. After years in America he had come home, bought a shop and farm, married, had children. We kept an account in his shop, and every Christmas he gave us a bottle of Redbreast and a tin of Jacob's figrolls.

'How is it, Michael, that you seem to be going home and we've never met in all this time at the sea?' my father asked.

'I guess it's because I just came down yesterday,' Michael Henry said as he put his small leather case in the overhead rack.

'How is it you're going home so soon?'

'I guess I thought the sea might do me some good but I only felt worse last night. I don't believe in shelling out good money to a hotel when you can be just as badly off at home. America teaches you those things.'

He sat the whole way home with my father. They talked of America and the war in Europe. Not many weeks later, in scarlet and white, I was to follow the priest round Michael Henry's coffin as he blessed it with holy water from the brass jar in my hands.

And suddenly the dead man climbing on the bus, the living girl asking me not to go to Sligo in the rain outside the hotel, I on the bus to Sligo to collect some letters, Barnaby and Bartleby, even now in their Dublin doorways patiently watching the day fade, seemed to be equally awash in time and indistinguishable, the same mute human presence beneath the unchanging sky, and for one moment I could not see how anyone could wish another pain. Were we not all waiting in the doorway?

xi

I went straight from the bus station to the Blue Anchor. I got the letters from Jimmy, saw some of the Pint Drinkers, including Old Jack. They were planning to take two barrels of stout out to Strandhill in a van one of these evenings, dig for clams, and have a party on the shore. Already it was a world I could no longer join. As we made our excuses for leaving, I to get the next bus back to Strandhill, Jimmy to meet his girl outside the cinema, Jack clapped us affectionately on the shoulders and said, 'Soon the pint days will be over. They'll have the leg-irons on yous in no time now.'

'Some other time we must make an evening of it,' Jimmy and his girl said as I left them at the cinema.

'Some other time,' I echoed but already my anxiety was returning, but as to why I was anxious or returning I did not know. The rain was heavier now and the drops fell like small yellow stones into the headlights of the bus. I hurried across the wet sand outside the hotel, and when I did not find her downstairs climbed to her room. I saw Costello's eyes follow me with open suspicion. When I knocked on her door there was no answer.

'Are you in, Kate?' I called softly and it was then I heard her low sobbing.

'I've just come back on the bus. I wondered if you'd like to come out for a drink?'

'No, thanks.' I could barely hear.

'I came back in the hope you'd come out. Are you sure you won't come?'

'No, thanks. I want to be alone.'

Slowly I retraced my steps down the narrow creaking corridor. There was nothing I could do but wait for morning.

xii

With a reluctance to face what the morning might turn out to be in the light of the evening before, I was late in coming down. The first thing that met my eyes was her luggage in the hallway. It was so plain and simple and brutal that I stopped short. She was leaving.

'I see Miss O'Mara decided to leave today after all,' I tried to say as casually as possible to Costello, who seemed to be as much on guard over the bags as in his usual place in the office.

'She told me to tell you that she's settled her account and is leaving,' he said in a tone which seemed to convey that I must have given her some good reason to leave with such suddenness.

She had had breakfast, and as I ate mine it grew clear that even outside the discomfort of remaining in Costello's hostility I had no longer any reason to stay, not indeed that there seemed now any reason to have ever come. A kind of anger against her for giving me no warning hardened my decision to leave at once. There was only one way she could leave, on the eleven o'clock bus, and I would leave with her on the same bus.

'I'd like to have the bill. I'm leaving,' I said to Costello, and as I was now meeting his aggression with aggression he did not trouble to answer. After pretending to consult some records, he presented me with the bill for the whole week. Hostile as I felt, I was forced to smile. 'But I've been here only four days.'

'You booked for a week.'

'Well, in that case, keep the room open for me,' I counted out what he had demanded. 'I'll probably come back tomorrow,' at which he exploded, 'No. Your type is not wanted again here,' and he slid the difference towards me.

'Thanks,' I said, but wishing now that I had paid in full, the morsel of my small victory distasteful.

The tide must be far out now I thought as I sat and listened to the pounding of the sea while waiting for the bus to turn at the cannon. It was a clear, fresh morning after the rain, only a few tattered shreds of white cloud in the blue sky. She did not come out until the bus was almost due. She was tense and looked as if she hadn't slept and was afraid when she saw me. Costello carried her bags, and as they prepared to wait together at a separate distance I decided to join them.

'I decided to leave too,' I said, and she then turned to Costello, 'You needn't wait any longer, Mr Costello. I'll be fine now. And are you sure you won't take something?'; and when he refused for what was obviously the second time he shook her hand warmly and went in. Even then she might not have spoken if I had not said, 'You should have let me know. It gave me no chance at all.'

'Does it matter so much?'

'No, not that much. But why make it more difficult than it has to be?'

'I'm sorry,' she said. 'I had to do it this way. I couldn't do it any other way. I didn't mean for you to leave at all.'

The bus was coming. As it was empty the conductor told us to take our bags on the bus, and we dumped them on the front seat. The waves seemed to pound louder than ever behind us above the creaky running of the bus.

'Did he charge you for the whole week?' I asked.

'I offered but he wouldn't take it.'

'The brute,' I smiled. 'He tried to charge me.'

I wanted to ask her about the evening before, about all that had gone before since we had first met at Nora Moran's, but I knew it was all hopeless, and I was blinded by no passion; I had not even that grace: at most it had been a seed, thrown on poor ground, half wishing it might come to something, in the wrong time of year. As if my silence was itself a question, she said as the bus came into Sligo, 'I can't explain anything that happened. I'll tell you some day but I can't now.'

'It's all right. Don't worry about it,' we were back in the

safety of the phrases that mean nothing. 'Anything worth explaining generally can't be explained anyhow.'

'We'll say goodbye here,' she said when we got off the bus. 'I'm sorry but I want to be alone.'

'Where'll you go?'

'To the hotel,' she motioned with her head. 'I'll get the two o'clock train. I hope you'll ring me when you get to Dublin. I won't be this way then.'

I turned away but saw her climb the steps, the glass door open and the doorman take her bags, a flash of light as the door closed. She would have a salad and a glass of wine and coffee, feel the expensive linen and smile at the waiter's smiles. She would be almost back in her own world before her train left, as I was almost back in mine.

How empty the doorways were, empty coffins stood on end.

Already Barnaby and Bartleby would be in their doorway in Abbey Street firmly fitting them till night, when they would silently leave.

All the people I had met at Nora Moran's, bowing and scraping and smiling in their doorways. Nora rushing from doorway to doorway, trying to bring all the doorways with her, 'I never feel easy without saying goodnight to mother'; Michael Henry climbing on the bus, 'I don't believe in shelling out good money to a hotel when you can be just as badly off at home. America teaches you those things,' the vivid green of the teal's feather in his hat as he disappeared into the years.

Kate O'Mara sitting in the big dining room of the hotel. The Pint Drinkers' Association, Jimmy McDermott, the last weeks in Sligo, the Kincora, the sea . . . everything seemed to be without shape. I understood nothing. Perhaps we had come to expect too much. Neither Barnaby nor Bartleby would tell. They didn't know. They just lived it.

I opened both my hands. They seemed quite empty. A clear morning came to me. It was on the edge of a town, close to the asylum, and a crowd of presumably harmless patients were hedging whitethorns along the main road, watched over by their male nurses. One patient seemed to be having a wonderful time. He lifted every branch he cut, and after a careful examination of each sprig began to laugh uproariously. I felt my empty hands were as worthy of as much uproarious mirth. But was not my present calm an equal and more courteous madness? and what I wanted anyhow was impossible—a real sanity—so maybe it had to seem like this impoverished madness.

I was free in the Sligo morning. I could do as I pleased. There were all sorts of wonderful impossibilities in sight. And the real difficulty was that the day was fast falling into its own night.

The Wine Breath

If I were to die, I'd miss most the mornings and the evenings, he thought as he walked the narrow dirt-track by the lake in the late evening, and then wondered if his mind was failing, for how could anybody think anything as stupid: being a man he had no choice, he was doomed to die; and being dead he'd miss nothing, being nothing. And it went against everything in his life as a priest.

The solid world, though, was everywhere around him. There was the lake, the road, the evening, and he was going to call on Gillespie. Gillespie was sawing. Gillespie was always sawing. The roaring rise-and-fall of the two-stroke stayed like a rent in the evening. And when he got to the black gate there was Gillespie, his overalled bulk framed in the short avenue of alders, and he was sawing not alders but beech, four or five tractorloads dumped in the front of the house. The priest put a hand to the black gate, bolted to the first of the alders, and was at once arrested by showery sunlight falling down the avenue. It lit up the one boot holding the length of beech in place, it lit the arms moving the blade slowly up and down as it tore through the beech, white chips milling out on the chain.

Suddenly, as he was about to rattle the gate loudly to see if this would penetrate the sawing, he felt himself (bathed as in a dream) in an incredible sweetness of light. It was the evening light on snow. The gate on which he had his hand vanished, the alders, Gillespie's formidable bulk, the roaring of the saw. He was in another day, the lost day of Michael Bruen's funeral nearly thirty years before. All was silent and still there. Slow feet crunched on the snow. Ahead, at the foot of the hill, the coffin rode slowly forward on shoulders, its brown varnish and metal trappings dull in the glittering snow, riding just below the long waste of snow eight or ten feet deep over the whole countryside. The long dark line of mourners following the coffin stretched away towards Oakport Wood in the pathway cut through the snow. High on Killeelan Hill the graveyard evergreens rose out of the snow. The graveyard wall was covered, the narrow path cut up the side of the hill stopping at the little gate deep in the snow. The coffin climbed with painful slowness, as if it might never reach the gate, often pausing for the bearers to be changed; and someone started to pray, the prayer travelling down the whole mile-long line of the mourners as they shuffled behind the coffin in the narrow tunnel cut in the snow.

It was the day in February 1947 that they buried Michael Bruen. Never before or since had he experienced the Mystery in such awesomeness. Now as he stood at the gate there was no awe or terror, only the coffin moving slowly towards the dark trees on the hill, the long line of the mourners, and everywhere the blinding white light, among the half-buried thorn bushes, and beyond Killeelan on the covered waste of Gloria Bog, on the sides of Slieve an Iarainn.

He did not know how long he had stood in that lost day, in that white light, probably for no more than a moment. He could not have stood the intensity for any longer. When he woke out of it the grey light of the alders had reasserted itself. His hand was still on the bar of the gate. Gillespie was still sawing, bent over the saw-horse, his boot on the length of beechwood, completely enclosed in the roaring rise-and-fall of the saw. The priest felt as vulnerable as if he had suddenly woken out of sleep, shaken and somewhat ashamed to have been caught asleep in the actual day and life, without any protection of walls.

He was about to rattle the gate again, feeling a washed-out parody of a child or old man on what was after all nothing more than a poor errand: to tell the Gillespies that a bed had at long last been made available in the Regional Hospital for the operation on Mrs Gillespie's piles, when his eyes were caught again by the quality of the light. It was one of those late October days, small white clouds drifting about the sun, and the watery light was shining down the alder rows to fall on the white chips of the beechwood strewn all about Gillespie, some inches deep. It was the same white light as the light on snow. As he watched the light went out on the beech chips, and it was the grey day again around Gillespie's sawing. It had been as simple as that. The suggestion of snow had been enough to plunge him in the lost day of Michael Bruen's funeral. Everything in that remembered day was so pure and perfect that he felt purged of all tiredness and bitterness, was, for a moment, eager to begin life again.

And, making sure that Gillespie hadn't noticed him at the gate, he turned back on the road. The bed wouldn't be ready for another week. The news could wait a day or more. Before leaving he stole a last look at the dull white ground about the sawhorse. The most difficult things seem always to lie closest to us, to lie always around our feet.

Ever since his mother's death he found himself stumbling into these dead days. Once, crushed mint in the garden had given him back a day he'd spent with her at the sea in such reality that he had been frightened, as if he'd suddenly fallen through time; it was as if the world of the dead was as available to him as the world of the living. It was also humiliating for him to realize that she must have been the mainspring of his days. And now that the mainspring was broken the hands were weakly falling here and falling there. Today there had been the sudden light on the bits of white beech. He'd not have noticed it if he hadn't been alone, if Gillespie had not been so absorbed in his sawing. Before there must have been some such simple trigger that he'd been too ashamed or bewildered to notice.

Stealthily and quickly he went down the dirt-track by the lake till he got to the main road. To the left was the church in a rookery of old trees, and behind it the house where he lived. Safe on the wide main road he let his mind go back to the beech chips. They rested there around Gillespie's large bulk, and paler still was the line of mourners following the coffin through the snow, a picture you could believe or disbelieve but not be in. In idle exasperation he began to count the trees in the hedge along the road as he walked: ash, green oak, whitethorn, ash; the last leaves a vivid yellow on the wild cherry, empty October fields in dull wet light behind the hedges. This, then, was the actual day, the only day that mattered, the day from which our salvation had to be won or lost: it stood solidly and impenetrably there, denying the weak life of the person, with nothing of the eternal other than it would dully endure, while the day set alight in his mind by the light of the white beech, though it had been nothing more than a funeral he had attended during a dramatic snowfall when a boy, seemed bathed in the eternal, seemed everything we had been taught and told of the world of God.

Dissatisfied, and feeling as tired again as he'd been on his way to Gillespie's, he did not go through the church gate with its circle and cross, nor did he call to the sexton locking up under the bellrope. In order to be certain of being left alone he went by the circular path at the side, round to the house, for a high laurel hedge hid the path from the graveyard and church. There he made coffee without turning on the light. Always when about to give birth or die cattle sought out a clean place in some corner of the field, away from the herd.

Michael Bruen had been a big kindly agreeable man, what was called a lovely man. His hair was a coarse grey. He wore loose-fitting tweeds with red cattleman's boots. When young he had been a policeman in Dublin. It was said he had either won or inherited money, and had come home to where he'd come from, to buy the big Crossna farm, to marry and grow rich.

He had a large family, and men were employed on the farm. The yard and its big outhouses with the red roofs rang with work: cans, machinery, raillery, the sliding of hooves, someone whistling. And within the house, away from the yard, was the enormous cave of a kitchen, the long table down its centre, the fireplace at its end, the plates and pots and presses along the walls, sides of bacon wrapped in gauze hanging from hooks in the ceiling, the whole room full of the excitement and bustle of women.

Often as a boy the priest had gone to Michael Bruen's on some errand for his father, a far smaller farmer than Michael. Once the beast was housed or the load emptied Michael would take him into the kitchen.

He remembered the last December evening well. He had driven over a white bullock. The huge fire of wood blazed all the brighter because of the frost.

'Give this man something,' Michael had led him. 'Something solid that'll warm the life back into him.'

'A cup of tea will do fine,' he had protested in the custom.

'Nonsense. Don't pay him the slightest attention. Empty bags can't stand.'

Eileen, the prettiest of Michael's daughters, laughed as she took down the pan. Her arms were white to the elbows with a fine dusting of flour.

'He'll remember this was a good place to come to when he has to start thinking about a wife,' Michael's words gave licence to general hilarity.

It was hard to concentrate on Michael's question about his father, so delicious was the smell of frying. The mug of steaming tea was put by his side. The butter melted on the fresh bread on the plate. There were sausages, liver, bacon, a slice of black-pudding and sweetest grisceens.

'Now set to,' Michael laughed. 'We don't want any empty bags leaving Bruen's.'

Michael came with him to the gate when he left. 'Tell your father it's ages since we had a drink in the Royal. And that if he doesn't search me out in the Royal the next Fair Day I'll have to go over and bate the lugs off him.' As he shook his hand in the half-light of the yard lamp it was the last time he was to see him alive. Before the last flakes had stopped falling, and when old people were searching back to 'the great snows when Count Plunkett was elected' to find another such fall Michael Bruen had died, and his life was already another such poor watermark of memory.

The snow lay eight feet deep on the roads, and dead cattle and sheep were found in drifts of fifteen feet in the fields. All of the people who hadn't lost sheep or cattle were in extraordinary good humour, their own ills buried for a time as deep as their envy of any other's good fortune in the general difficulty of the snow. It took days to cut a way out to the main road, the snow having to be cut in blocks breast-high out of a face of frozen snow. A wild cheer went up as the men at last cut through to the gang digging in from the main road. Another cheer greeted the first van to come in, Doherty's bread van, and it had hardly died when the hearse came with the coffin for Michael Bruen. That night they cut the path up the side of Killeelan Hill and found the family headstone beside the big yew just inside the gate and opened the grave. They hadn't finished digging when the first funeral bell came clearly over the snow the next day to tell them that the coffin had started on its way.

The priest hadn't thought of the day for years or of Michael Bruen till he had stumbled into it without warning by way of the sudden light on the beech chips. It did not augur well. There were days, especially of late, when he seemed to be lost in dead days, to see time present as a flimsy accumulating tissue over all the time that was lost. Sometimes he saw himself as an old man that boys were helping down to the shore, restraining the tension of their need to laugh as they pointed out a rock in the path he seemed about to stumble over, and then they had to lift their eyes and smile apologetically to the passersby while he stood staring out to sea, having forgotten all about the rock in his path. 'It's this way we're going,' he felt the imaginary tug on his sleeve, and he was drawn again into the tortuous existence of the everyday, away from the eternal of the sea or the lost light on frozen snow across Killeelan Hill.

Never before though had he noticed anything like the beech chips. There was the joy of holding what had eluded him for so long, in its amazing simplicity: but mastered knowledge was soon no knowledge, unless it opened, became part of a greater knowledge, and what did the beech chips do but turn back to his own death.

Like the sudden snowfall and Michael Bruen's burial his life had been like any other, except to himself, and then only in odd visions of it, as a lost life. When it had been agreeable and equitable he had no vision of it at all.

The country childhood. His mother and father. The arrival at the shocking knowledge of birth and death. His attraction to the priesthood as a way of vanquishing death and avoiding birth. O hurry it, he thought. There is not much to a life. Many have it. There is not enough room. His father and mother were old when they married, and he was 'the fruit of old things', he heard derisively. His mother had been a seamstress. He could still see the needle flashing in her strong hands, that single needle flash composed of thousands of hours.

'His mother had the vocation for him,' perhaps she had, perhaps all the mothers of the country had, it had so passed into the speech of the country, in all the forms of both beatification and derision; and it was out of fear of death he became a priest, which becomes in its time the fear of life, and wasn't it natural to turn back to the mother in this fear: she was older than fear, having given him his life, and who would give a life if they knew its end. There was then his father's death, the father accepting it as he had accepted all poor fortune all his life long, as his due, refusing to credit the good.

And afterwards his mother sold the land to 'Horse' Mc-Laughlin and came to live with him, and was happy. She attended all the Masses and Devotions, took messages, and she sewed, though she had no longer any need, linen for the altar, soutanes and surplices, his shirts and all her own clothes. Sometimes her concern for him irritated him to exasperation but he hardly ever let it show. He was busy with the many duties of a priest. The fences on the past and future were secure. He must have been what is called happy, and there was a whole part of his life that without his knowing had come to turn to her for its own expression.

He discovered it when she began her death. He came home one summer evening to find all the lights in the house on. She was in the livingroom, in the usual chair. The table was piled high with dresses. Round the chair was a pile of rags. She did not look up when he entered, her still strong hands tearing apart a herring-bone skirt she had made only the year before.

'What on earth are you doing, Mother?' he caught her by the hands when she didn't answer.

'It's time you were up for Mass,' she said.

'What are you doing with all your dresses?'

'What dresses?'

'All the dresses you've just been tearing up.'

'I don't know anything about dresses,' and then he saw there was something wrong. She made no resistance when he led her up the stairs.

For some days she seemed absent and confused but, though he watched her carefully, she was otherwise very little different from her old self, and she did not appear ill. Then he came home one evening to find her standing like a child in the middle of the room, surrounded by an enormous pile of rags. She had taken up from where she'd been interrupted at the herring-bone skirt, and had torn up every dress or article of clothing she had ever made. After his initial shock he did the usual and sent for the doctor.

'I'm afraid it's just the onset of senility,' the doctor said.

'It's irreversible?'

The doctor nodded, 'It very seldom takes such a violent form, but that's what it is. She'll have to be looked after.' And with a sadness that part of his life was over, he took her to the Home and saw her settled there.

She recognized him when he visited her there the first year, but without excitement, as if he was already far away; and then the day came when he had to admit that she no longer knew who he was, had become like a dog kennelled out too long. He was with her when she died. She'd turned her face toward him. There came what seemed a light of recognition in the eyes like a last glow of a match before it goes out, and then she died.

There was nothing left but his own life. There had been nothing but that all along, but it had been obscured, comfortably obscured.

He turned on the radio.

A man had lost both legs in an explosion. There was violence on the night-shift at Ford's. The pound had steadied towards the close but was still down on the day.

Letting his fingers linger on the knob he turned it off. The disembodied voice on the air was not unlike the lost day he'd stumbled into through the light on the beech chips, except it had nothing of its radiance—the funeral during the years he must have carried it around with him had lost the sheltered burden of the everyday, had become light as the air in all the clarity of light. It was all timeless, and seemed at least a promise of the eternal.

He went to draw the curtain. She had made the red curtain too with its pale lining but hadn't torn it. How often must she have watched the moonlight on the still headstones beyond the laurel, as it lay evenly on them this night. She had been afraid of ghosts: old priests who had lived in this house, who through whiskey or some other ill had neglected to say some Mass for the dead—and because of the neglect the soul for whom the Mass should have been offered was forced to linger beyond its time in Purgatory—and the priest guilty of the omission could him-

105

self not be released until the living priest had said the Mass, and was forced to come at midnight to the house in all his bondage until that Mass was said.

'They must have been all good priests, Mother. Good steady old fellows like myself. They never come back,' he used to assure her. He remembered his own idle words as he drew the curtain, lingering as much over the drawing of the curtain as he had lingered over the turning off of the radio. He would be glad of a ghost tonight, be glad of any visitation from beyond the walls of sense.

He took up the battered and friendly missal, which had been with him all his adult life, to read the office of the day. On bad days he kept it till late, the familiar words that changed with the changing year, that he had grown to love, and were as well his daily duty. It must be surely the greatest grace of life, the greatest freedom, to have to do what we love because it is also our duty. But he wasn't able to read on this evening among the old familiar words for long. An annoyance came between him and the page, the Mass he had to repeat every day, the Mass in English. He wasn't sure whether he hated it or the guitar-playing priests more. It was humiliating to think that these had never been such a scourge when his mother had been alive. Was his life the calm vessel it had seemed, dully setting out and returning from the fishing grounds. Or had he been always what he seemed now. 'Oh yes. There you go again,' he heard the familiar voice in the empty room. 'Complaining about the Mass in the vernacular. When you prefer the common names of flowers to their proper names,' and the sharp, energetic, almost brutal laugh. It was Peter Joyce, he was not dead. Peter Joyce had risen to become a bishop at the other end of the country, to become an old friend that he no longer saw.

'But they are more beautiful. Dog rose, wild woodbine, buttercup, daisy. . . .'

He heard his own protest. It was in a hotel that they used to go to every summer on the Atlantic, a small hotel where you could read after dinner without fear of a rising roar from the bar beginning to outrival the Atlantic by ten o'clock.

'And, no doubt, the little rose of Scotland, sharp and sweet and breaks the heart,' he heard his friend quote maliciously. 'And it's not the point. The reason that names of flowers must be in Latin is that when flower lovers meet they know what they are talking about, no matter whether they're French or Greeks or Arabs. They have a universal language.'

'I prefer the humble names, no matter what you say.'

'Of course you do. And it's parochial sentimentalists like yourself who prefer the *smooth sowthistle* to *Sonchus oleraceus* that's the whole cause of your late lamented Mass in Latin disappearing. I have no sympathy with you. You people tire me.'

The memory of that truculent argument dispelled completely his annoyance, as its simple logic had once taken his breath away, but he was curiously tired after the vividness of the recall. It was only by a sheer act of will, sometimes having to count the words, that he was able to finish his office. 'I know one thing, Peter Joyce. I know that I know nothing,' he murmured when he finished. But when he looked at the room about him he could hardly believe it was so empty and dead and dry, the empty chair where she should be sewing, the oaken table with the scattered books, the clock on the mantel. And wildly and aridly he wanted to curse. But his desire to curse was as unfair as life. He had not wanted it.

And then, quietly, he saw that he had a ghost all right, one that he had been walking around with for a long time, a ghost he had not wanted to recognize—his own death. He might as well get to know him well, he would never leave now. He was in the room, and had no mortal shape. Absence does not cast a shadow.

All there was was the white light of the lamp on the open book, on the white marble; the brief sun of God on beechwood, and the sudden light of that glistening snow, and the timeless mourners moving towards the yews on Killeelan Hill almost thirty years ago. It was as good a day as any, if there ever could be a good day to go.

And somewhere, outside this room that was an end, he knew that a young man not unlike he had been once stood on a granite step and listened to the doorbell ring, smiled as he heard a woman's footsteps come down the hallway, ran his fingers through his hair, and turned the bottle of white wine he held in his hands completely around as he prepared to enter a pleasant and uncomplicated evening, feeling himself immersed in time without end.

Along the Edges

EVENING

'I must go now.' She tried to rise from the bed.

'Stay.' His arms about her pale shoulders held her back as she pressed upwards with her hands. 'Let me kiss you there once more.'

'Don't be silly,' she laughed and fell back into his arms. 'I have to go.' Her body trembled with low laughter as he went beneath the sheet to kiss her; and then they stretched full length against one another, kissing over and back on the mouth, in a last grasping embrace.

'I wish I could eat and drink you.'

'Then I'd be gone,' she pushed him loose with her palms. They both rose and dressed quickly.

'I'll leave you home. It's too late for you to go alone.' Lately she had seemed to want to assert their separateness after each lovemaking, when she should be the more his.

'All right, but I don't mind,' she said, a seeming challenge in her eyes.

'Besides I want to,' he leaned to kiss her on the side of the throat as she drew on her jacket. They stole down the stairs, and outside he held the door firmly until the catch clicked quietly behind them. The fading moonlight was weak on the leaves of the single laurel in the front garden, and he grew uneasy at the apparent reluctance with which she seemed to give him her gloved hand on the pavement, with the way she hurried, their separate footsteps loud in the silence of the sleeping suburbs.

They'd met just after broken love affairs, and had drifted casually into going out together two or three evenings every week. They went to cinemas or dancehalls or restaurants, to the races at Leopardstown or the Park, making no demands on one another, sharing only one another's pleasures, making love together as on this night in his student's room.

Sensing her hard separateness in their separate footsteps as they walked towards her home in the sleeping suburbs, he began to feel that by now there should be more between them than this sensual ease. Till now, for him, the luxury of this ease had been perfect. This uncomplicated pleasure seemed the very fullness of life, seemed all that life could yearn towards, and yet it could not go on forever. There comes a point in all living things when they must change or die, and maybe they had passed that point already without noticing, and that already he had lost her, when he was longing to draw closer.

'When will we meet again?' he asked her as usual at the gate before she went in.

'When do you want?' she asked as usual.

'Saturday, at eight, outside the Metropole.'

'Saturday—at eight, then,' she agreed.

There was no need to seek for more. His anxiety had been groundless. Wednesdays and Saturdays were always given. No matter how hard the week was he had always Saturdays and Wednesdays to look forward to: he could lean upon their sensual ease and luxury as reliably as upon a drug. Now that Saturday was once more promised his life was perfectly arranged. With all the casualness of the self-satisfied male, he kissed her goodnight and it caused her to look sharply at him before she went in, but he noticed nothing. He waited until he heard the latch click and then went whistling home through the empty silent streets just beginning to grow light.

That next Saturday he stayed alone in the room, studying by the light of a bulb fixed on a chianti bottle, the texts and diagrams spread out on newspaper that shielded his arms from the cold of the marble top that had once been a washstand, the faded velvet curtain drawn on the garden and hot day outside, on cries of the ice-cream wagons, on the long queues within the city for buses to the sea, on the sea of Dollymount and the swimmers going in off the rocks, pleasures sharpened a hundred-fold by the drawn curtain. Finally, late in the afternoon, when he discovered that he had just reached the bottom of a page without taking in a single sentence, he left the room and went down to the front. At the corner shop he bought an orange and sat on a bench. The sea lay dazzling in the heat out past the Bull and Howth Head. An old couple and a terrier with a news-paper in his mouth went past him as he peeled the orange. Music came from a transistor somewhere. Exams should be held in winter, he thought tiredly, for he seemed to be looking at the people walking past him and lolling on other benches or on the thin grass, on the shimmering sea itself, and the dark buildings across the bay, as if through plate glass.

Still, at eight o'clock she would come to him, out of the mill-ing crowds about the Metropole, her long limbs burning nakedly beneath the swinging folds of the brown dress that hid them and flaunted them, the face that came towards him and then drew back as she laughed, and he would begin to live again. He had all that forgetting to go towards, the losing of the day in all the sweetness of her night. He rose, threw the orange peel into a wire basket, and walked back to the room. He imagined he must have been working for about an hour when he heard the heavy knocker of the front door go; but when he looked at his watch he found that he had been working already for more than two hours, which must be the greater part of happiness.

After the knocking, he listened as the door was opened, and heard voices—the landlord's, probably the vegetable man or the coal man—but went quite still as steps came up the stairs towards the door of the room, the landlord's steps because of the heavy breathing. A knock came on the door, and the fat, little old landlord put his head in, stains of egg yolk on his lapels. 'A visitor for you,' he whispered and winked.

She stood below in the hallway beside the dark bentwood coat rack, her legs crossed as if for a casual photo, arms folded, a tense smile fixed on her face, her hair brushed high. She had never come to the house on her own before. Was something wrong? Or had she grown impatient waiting to meet him at the Metropole and come to him early?

'Thanks,' she said to the landlord when he came down.

'Won't you come up?' he called from the head of the stairs.

The landlord made a face and winked again as she climbed.

'I'm sorry coming like this,' she said.

'No, that doesn't matter,' he said as he closed the door. 'I was just about to get ready to go to meet you. This way we can have even more time together.'

'It's not that,' she said quickly. 'I came round to see if you'd mind putting the evening off.'

'Why, is there something wrong?'

'No. It's just that Margaret has come up of a sudden from the country.'

'That's your friend from school days?'

'Yes. She hardly ever comes up. And I thought you wouldn't mind giving the evening up so that we could go out together.'

'Did she not tell you she was coming up?' The whole long-looked-forward-to balm of the evening was threatened by this whim or accident.

'No. She came on a chance. Someone was coming up and offered her a lift.'

'And she expects you to drop everything and dance attendance on her?'

'She doesn't expect anything,' she met his annoyance with her own.

'All I can say is that it's very poor. You must have cared very little about the evening if you can change it that quickly.'

'Well, if you're that huffed about it we can go through with the evening. I didn't think you'd mind.'

'Where is this Margaret?'

'She's outside. Why do you want to know?'

'I suppose I should pay my respects and let the pair of you away...'

'Don't put yourself out.'

'It'll be a pleasure,' but then his anger broke before he opened the door. 'If that's all our going out means to you we might as well forget the whole thing.'

'What do you mean?' she asked.

'We might as well break the whole thing off,' he said less certainly.

'That can be easily arranged.'

'It might be arranged for you.' The door was open and they both came downstairs in silent anger.

Outside, Margaret was leaning against the railing by the bus top. She was a large country girl, with a mane of black hair and board athlete's shoulders. The three made polite, awkward conversation that did not cover over the tenseness till the bus came.

'I hope you have a nice evening,' he said as they boarded the bus.

'That's what we intend,' her lovely face was unflinching, but Margaret waved. He watched them take a seat together on the lower deck and waited to see if they would look back, but they did not.

Rattling coins, he went towards the telephone box at the end of the road to ring round to see if any of his friends were free for the evening.

They did not meet again till two Saturdays later, at the Metropole, as usual at eight. She had on a floppy blue hat and dark glasses. Her summer dress was sleeveless, and she had a race card in her long gloved hands.

113

'You must have just come from the races.'

'I was at the Park. I even won some money,' she smiled her old roguish smile.

'You must be hungry then. Why don't we go somewhere nice to eat?'

'That's fine with me,' she said with all her mocking brightness. 'I can take you—this evening—with the winnings.'

'If that suits you. I have money too.'

'You took long enough in calling,' she said with a flash of real resentment.

'It didn't seem that it'd make much difference to you. It'd be nice for me to think I was wrong, but that's how it seemed when I thought it out.'

'Where are we going?' she stopped, and that they were adversaries now was in the open.

'To Bernardo's. We always had good times there. Even coming from the races you look very beautiful,' he said by way of appeasement.

The resturant was just beginning to fill. The blindman was playing the piano at its end, his white stick leaning against the dark varnish. They ate in tenseness and mostly silence, the piano thumping indifferently away. She had never looked so beautiful; it was like an old tune, now that he was about to lose her. It was as if this evening was an echo of a darker evening and was uniting with it to try to break him.

'You're not eating much,' she said when she saw him struggle with the veal.

'It must be the damned exam,' he said. 'It's starting next week. And, after all, I wasn't at the races.'

'That's true,' she laughed.

'I'm sorry about that ridiculous fuss I made a few weeks back,' he said openly.

'It's all right. It's all over now.'

'Do you think you'll be able to come back with me this evening?' For a wild sensual moment he hoped everything would suddenly be as it had been before.

'Is it for—the usual?' she asked slowly.

'I suppose.'

'No,' she shook her head, and it sounded like a more gentle toll of another No.

'Why?'

'I don't see any point. Do you?'

'We've often . . . many times before.'

'We've gone on that way for too long,' she said.

'But I love you. And I thought—when things are more settled —we might be married.'

'No,' she was looking at him with affection and trying to speak softly and slowly. 'You must know that the only time things are settled, if they are ever settled, is *now*. And I've had some hard thinking to do since that last evening. You were quite right to be angry. If I was seriously interested in you I'd not have broken the date for someone coming casually to town. There was a time I thought I was getting involved with you, but then you didn't seem interested, and women are practical. I'm very fond of you, and we've had good times, and maybe the good times just went on for too long, when we just should have had a romp, and let it go,' she spoke as if it already belonged to a life that was over.

'Is there no hope, no hope at all, that it might change?' he asked with nothing more than an echo of desperation.

Through the sensual caresses, laughter, evenings of pleasure, the instinct had been beginning to assemble a dream, a hope; soon, little by little, without knowing, he would have woken to find that he had fallen in love. We assemble a love as we assemble our life and grow so absorbed in the assembling that we wake in terror at the knowledge that all that we have built is terminal, that in our pain we must undo it again.

There had been that moment too that might have been grasped at the flood, and had not, and love had died—she had admitted as much. It would have led on to what? To happiness, for a while, or the absence of this present sense of loss, or to some other sense of loss. . . .

He thought he saw that moment, as well that moment now as any other: an evening in O'Connell Street, a Saturday evening like any other, full of the excitement of the herding. She had taken his arm.

'My young sister is to be engaged tomorrow. Why don't we drive up? There's to be a party. And afterwards we could have the weekend on our own,' and when he answered, 'It's the one weekend I can't,' and started to explain, he saw the sudden glow go from her face; an impoverishment of calculation replaced it that had made him momentarily afraid. Anyhow, it was all evening now. That crossroad at which they had actually separated had been passed long before in the day.

'No,' she said gently. 'And you'd not be so reckless if I'd said Yes. We were both more in love with the idea of falling in love, of escaping.'

'Still it's no fun walking round the world on your own.'

'It's not so bad as being with someone you can't stand after the pleasure has worn off,' she said as if she were looking past the evening.

'I give up,' he said and called for the bill.

'Ring me sometime,' she said as she got on the bus outside.

'Right, then,' he waved and knew neither of them would. They had played at a game of life, and had not fallen, and were now as indifferent to one another, outside the memory of pleasure, as if they were both already dead to one another. If they were not together in the evening how could they ever have been so in the morning. . . .

And if she had come to him instead of leaving him, those limbs would never reach whomever they were going to. . . .

And why should we wish the darkness harm, it is our element; or curse the darkness because we are doomed to love in it, and die. . . .

And those that move along the edges can see it so until they fall.

MORNING

'What does your friend do for a living?' the man asked the blonde woman in front of him after Marion, an enormous ungainly girl, had gone to the Ladies in Bernardo's.

'She's not a friend. In fact, she's more than a friend. She's a client. She's a star. A pop star,' The woman smiled as she drew slowly on her cigarette. 'You're behind the times. You see, I'm here to bring you up to date.'

'But how can she be a pop star?'

'You mean because she's ugly? That doesn't matter. That helps. The public's tired of long, pale, beautiful slenders. Ugliness and energy—that's what's wanted now. And she has a good voice. She can belt them out.'

'Does she have men friends and all that?'

'As many as she wants. Proposals. Everything a woman's supposed to want.'

'She's certainly not what you'd call beautiful.'

'Publicity makes her beautiful. It moves her closer to the sun. In fact, it is the sun and still has its worshippers.'

'It doesn't make her beautiful to me,' the man said doggedly, 'though I think you're beautiful.'

'What *is* beauty? A good clothes rack or a good flesh rack? I don't know.'

'Whatever it is, you have it.' He changed, 'It doesn't look as if Peter will come back now.'

'No,' she said. 'Peter isn't trustworthy. I wish they'd let the blindman go home,' she said as he struck up another number on the piano.

'I suppose, for them, it's the hopeful hours,' the man referred to the large noisy table in the centre of the restaurant. They had come from a party, and had bribed the blindman to play on after he had risen about midnight to catch his usual garage bus to Inchicore.

'Do you have anything to do with Peter?'

'How?' she asked sharply.

'Sleep with him?'

She laughed. 'I've never even thought of Peter that way. He's a contact. In the trade,' and without warning she leaned across the table and placed the burning tip of the cigarette against the back of the man's hand.

'What did you want to do that for?' he asked angrily.

'I felt like it. I suppose I should be sorry.'

'No,' he changed. 'Not if you come home with me.'

'To sleep with you?' she parodied.

'That would be best of all but it's not important. We can spend the morning together,' he said eagerly.

'All right,' she nodded.

They were both uneasy after the agreement. They had left one level and had not entered any other.

'Do you think I should go to see if anything's the matter with Marion?'

'Maybe. Wait a little,' he said.

Marion was pale when she came back. 'I'm afraid I'm not used to the wine,' she apologized.

'I'm sorry, but we can go now. Do you think you will be all right?'

'I'll be fine,' she said.

'Anyhow, you'll both see Peter tomorrow. He said he'd definitely be at the reception.'

The last thing their eyes rested on before they went through the door the Italian manager was holding open was the blind-man's cane leaning against the side of the piano.

'Do you think they'll make the poor man play all night?' she asked.

'He seems satisfied. I even heard them arranging for a taxi to take him home. I suppose we too should be thinking of a taxi.'

'I'd rather walk, if that's all right.'

They walked slowly towards the hotel. The night was fine but without moon or stars. Just before they got to the hotel, the man shook hands with Marion, and the two women walked together to the hotel door. They stood a while in conversation there before the star went in and the blonde woman turned back towards the man.

'It always makes me uncomfortable. Being part of the couple, leaving the single person alone,' he said.

'The single person is usually glad to be left alone.'

'I know that but it doesn't stop the feeling,' it was the same feeling one got passing hushed hospitals late at night.

'Anyhow, you've had your wish. We're together,' the woman said, and they kissed for the first time. They crossed to the taxi rank facing the railings of the Green, and they did not speak in the taxi. What hung between them might be brutal and powerful, but it was as frail as the flesh out of which it grew, for any endurance. They had chosen one another because of the empty night, and the wrong words might betray them early, making one hateful to the other; but even the right words, if there were right words, had not the power to force it. It had to grow or wither like a wild flower. What they needed most was patience, luck, and that twice-difficult thing, to be lucky in one another, and at the same time, and to be able to wait for that time.

'Will I switch on the light?' he asked her as he let her into the flat.

'Whatever you like.'

'Then I'd rather not.'

After they had kissed he said, 'There's my room and the spare room. I don't mind if you think it too soon and use the spare room.'

'Wait,' she said softly, and her arms leaned heavily round his shoulders, as if she had forgotten him, and was going over her life to see if she could gather it into this one place. Suddenly she felt him trembling. She pulled him towards her.

'Do you bring many people back like this?' she asked close to morning, almost proprietorially.

'No. Not for ages.'

'Why?'

'First you have to find a person who'll consent,' he half joked. 'And there's not much use after a while unless there seems a chance of something more.'

'Of what?'

'Of it going on, I suppose.'

There was a silence in which a moth blundering about the half-darkness overhead was too audible.

'And you, have you men?' he asked awkwardly.

'No. Until recently I had one man.'

'What happened?'

'Nothing. He was married. It sounds like a record.'

'It's all a record, but it seems the only record worth hearing.'

And it only takes one person to make it new again, the quality of the making being all that mattered.

'Well, the poor quality record went this way. The man in question had a quite awful dilemma, and he suffered, how he suffered, especially with me. You see, he was torn between his wife and myself, and he could not make up his mind. Women are, I think, more primal than men. They don't bother too much about who pays the bill as long as they get what they want. So I gave him an ultimatum. And when he still couldn't make up his mind I left him. That must sound pretty poor stuff.'

'No. It sounds true.'

That hard as porcelain singleness of women, seeming sometimes to take pleasure in cruelty, was part of their beauty too.

'Would you like to be married?'

'Yes. And you?'

'I suppose I would.'

'You know that speech about those that are married or kind to their friends. They become olives, pomegranate, mulberry, flowers, precious stones, eminent stars.'

120

'I'd rather stay as I am,' she laughed.

'But you still see yourself at it.'

'That's just self-consciousness.'

'And pain isn't pain. It's just morbid organs monitoring distress. It's all wrong.'

'Well, let it be wrong then. It's all we have and that just happens to be the way we have it. We didn't choose it. Any more than those before us, or those that may come after us.'

When they rose and washed in the flat in all its daylight, it seemed as if it was not only a new day but the beginning of a new life. The pictures, the plates, the table in its stolidity seemed to have been set askew by the accidental night, to want new shapes, to look comical in their old places. The books on the wall, the hours spent with them, seemed to have belonged to an old relative to whom one did not even owe a responsibility of affection. Gaily one could pick or discard among them, choosing only those useful to the new. For, like a plant, the old outer leaves would have to lie withered for new green shoots to push upwards at the heart.

'What are you thinking?'

'Nothing much. Of another morning. A Paris morning, opening shutters, a water truck was going past, and behind came four Algerians with long-handled brooms.'

'Were you alone or with someone?' he was ashamed of the first pang of irrational jealousy, and it was as if some old record that should be drowned out was starting up again in spite of everything.

'Actually, I was alone. I suppose one is mostly alone in those mornings,' her gravity as much as a small child's took all the light to itself.

They had come from four separate people, two men and two women, lying together in two separate nights; and those two nights were joined in the night they had left, had grown into the morning.

She was not garlanded by farms or orchards, by any house

121

by the sea, by neither judges nor philosophers. She stood as she was, belonging to the morning, as they both hoped to belong to the evening. They could not possess the morning, no more than they could disagree with it or go against its joy.

She was wearing what she wore at the dinner while the blindman played, a dress of blue denim, buttoned down the front, and on her stockingless feet were thonged sandals.

'What are you going to do today?'

'I have to go to the hotel, and then to the reception. I suppose we'll see the busy Peter there. After that I'm free. And you?'

'I'm free all day.'

'Maybe we'll begin to learn a little more about one another then.'

'As long as we know it'll be more of nothing. We know hardly anything now and we may never be as well off.' They would have to know that they could know nothing to go through the low door of love, the door that was the same doorway between the self and the other everywhere.

'Well, anyhow we have to face the day,' she said, dispelling it in one movement; and they took one another's hands as they went to meet the day, the day already following them, and all about them.

Gold Watch

It was in Grafton Street we met, aimlessly strolling in one of the lazy lovely Saturday mornings in spring, the week of work over, the weekend still as fresh as the bunch of anemones that seemed the only purchase in her cane shopping basket.

'What a lovely surprise,' I said.

I was about to take her hand when a man with an armload of parcels parted us as she was shifting the basket to her other hand, and we withdrew out of the pushing crowds into the comparative quiet of Harry Street. We had not met since we had graduated in the same law class from University College five years before. I had heard she'd become engaged to the medical student she used to knock around with, and had gone into private practice down the country, perhaps waiting for him to graduate.

'Are you up for the weekend or on holiday or what?' I asked.

'No. I work here now.' She named a big firm that specialised in tax law. 'I felt I needed a change.'

She was wearing a beautiful suit, the colour of oatmeal, the narrow skirt slit from the knee. The long gold hair of her student days was drawn tightly into a neat bun at the back.

'You look different but as beautiful as ever,' I said. 'I thought you'd be married by now.'

'And do you still go home every summer?' she countered, perhaps out of confusion.

'It doesn't seem as if I'll ever break that bad habit.'

We had coffee in Bewley's—the scent of the roasting beans blowing through the vents out onto Grafton Street forever mixed through the memory of that morning—and we went on to spend

the whole idle day together until she laughingly and firmly returned my first hesitant kiss; and it was she who silenced my
even more fumbled offer of marriage several weeks later. 'No,'
she said. 'I don't want to be married. But we can move in together and see how it goes. If it doesn't turn out well we can split and
there'll be no bitterness.'

And it was she who found the flat in Hume Street, on the top
floor of one of those old Georgian houses in off the Green, within
walking distance of both our places of work. There was extraordinary peace and loveliness in those first weeks together that I
will always link with those high-ceilinged rooms—the eager rush
of excitement I felt as I left the office at the end of the day; the
lingering in the streets to buy some offering of flowers or fruit or
wine or a bowl and once one copper pan; and then rushing up the
stairs to call her name, the emptiness of those same rooms when
I'd find she hadn't got home yet.

'Why are we so happy?' I would ask.

'Don't worry it,' she always said, and sealed my lips with a
touch.

That early summer we drove down one weekend to the small
town in Kilkenny where she had grown up, and above her father's bakery we slept in separate rooms. That Sunday a whole
stream of relatives—aunts, cousins, two uncles, with trams of
children—kept arriving at the house. Word had gone out, and
they had plainly come to look me over. This brought the tension
between herself and her schoolteacher mother into open quarrel
late that evening after dinner. Her father sat with me in the
front room, cautiously kind, sipping whiskey as we measured
each careful cliché, listening to the quarrel slow and rise and
crack in the far-off kitchen. I had found the sense of comfort
and space charming for a time, but by the time we left I, too,
was beginning to find the small town claustrophobic.

'Unfortunately the best part of these visits is always the leaving,' she said as we drove away. 'After a while away you're lured
into thinking that the next time will somehow be different, but it
never is.'

'Wait—wait until you see my place. Then you may well think differently. At least your crowd made an effort. And your father is a nice man.'

'And yet you keep going back to the old place?'

'That's true. That's something in my own nature. I have to face that now. It's just easier for me to go back than to cut. That way I don't feel any guilt. I don't feel anything.'

I knew myself too well. There was more caution than any love or charity in my habitual going home. It was unattractive and it had been learned in the bitter school of my ungiving father. I would fall into no guilt, and I was already fast outwearing him. For a time, it seemed, I could outstare the one eye of nature.

I had even waited for love, if love this was; for it was happiness such as I had never known.

'You see, I waited long enough for you,' I said as we drove away from her Kilkenny town. 'I hope I can keep you now.'

'If it wasn't me it would be some other. My mother will never understand that. You might as well say I waited long enough for you.'

The visit we made to my father, some weeks later, quickly turned to disaster far worse than I had at the very worst envisaged. I saw him watch us as I got out of the car to open the iron gate under the yew, but instead of coming out to greet us he withdrew into the shadows of the hallway. It was my stepmother, Rose, who came out to the car when we both got out and were opening the small garden gate. We had to follow her smiles and trills of speech all the way into the kitchen to find my father, who was seated in the car chair, and he did not rise to take our hands.

After a lunch that was silent, in spite of several shuttlecocks of speech Rose tried to keep in the air, he said as he took his hat from the sill, 'I want to ask you about these walnuts,' and I followed him out into the fields. The mock orange was in blossom, and it was where the mock orange stood out from the clump of egg bushes that he turned suddenly and said, 'What age is your intended? She looks well on her way to forty.'

'She's the same age as I am,' I said blankly. I could hardly think, caught between the shock and pure amazement.

'I don't believe it,' he said.

'You don't have to, but we were in the same class at university.' I turned away.

Walking with her in the same field close to the mock orange tree late that evening, I said, 'Do you know what my father said to me?'

'No,' she said happily. 'But from what I've seen I don't think anything will surprise me.'

'We were walking just here,' I began, and repeated what he'd said. When I saw her go still and pale I knew I should not have spoken.

'He said I look close to forty,' she repeated. 'I have to get out of this place.'

'Stay this one night,' I begged. 'It's late now. We'd have to stay in a hotel. It'd be making it into too big of a production. You don't ever have to come back again, if you don't want to, but stay the night. It'll be easier.'

'I'll not want to come back,' she said as she agreed to see out this one night.

'But why do you think he said it?' I asked her later when we were both quiet, sitting on a wall at the end of the Big Meadow, watching the shadows of the evening deepen between the beeches, putting off the time when we'd have to go into the house, not unlike two grown children.

'Is there any doubt? Out of simple hatred. There's no living with that kind of hatred.'

'We'll leave first thing in the morning,' I promised.

'And why did you,' she asked, tickling my throat with a blade of ryegrass, 'say I was if anything too beautiful?'

'Because it's true. It makes you public and it's harder to live naturally. You live in too many eyes—in envy or confusion or even simple admiration, it's all the same. I think it makes it harder to live luckily.'

'But it gives you many advantages.'

'If you make use of those advantages, you're drawn even deeper in. And of course I'm afraid it'll attract people who'll try to steal you from me.'

'That won't happen.' She laughed. She'd recovered all her natural good spirits. 'And now I suppose we better go in and face the ogre. We have to do it sooner or later and it's getting chilly.'

My father tried to be very charming when we went in, but there was a false heartiness in the voice that made clear that it grew out of no well meaning. He felt he'd lost ground, and was now trying to recover it far too quickly. Using silence and politeness like a single weapon, we refused to be drawn in; and when pressed to stay the next morning, we said unequivocally that we had to be back. Except for one summer when I went to work in England, the summer my father married Rose, I had always gone home to help at the hay; and after I entered the civil service I was able to arrange holidays so that they fell around haytime. They had come to depend on me, and I liked the work. My father had never forgiven me for taking my chance to go to university. He had wanted me to stay at home to work the land. I had always fought his need to turn my refusal into betrayal. And by going home each summer I felt I was affirming that the great betrayal was not mine but nature's own.

I had arranged the holidays to fall at haytime that year as I had all the years before I met her, but since he'd turned to me at the mock orange tree I was no longer sure I had to go. I was no longer free, since in everything but name our life together seemed growing into marriage. It might even make him happy for a time if he could call it my betrayal.

'I don't know what to do,' I confessed to her a week before I was due to take holidays. 'They've come to depend on me for the hay. Everything else they can manage themselves. I know they'll expect me.'

'What do you want to do?'

'I suppose I'd prefer to go home—that's if you don't mind.'

'Why do you prefer?'

'I like working at the hay. You come back to the city feeling fit and well.'

'Is that the real reason?'

'No. It's something that might even be called sinister. I've gone home for so long that I'd like to see it through. I don't want to be blamed for finishing it, though it'll finish soon, with or without me. But this way I don't have to think about it.'

'Maybe it would be kinder, then, to do just that, and take the blame.'

'It probably would be kinder, but kindness died between us so long ago that it doesn't enter into it.'

'So there was some kindness?'

'When I was younger,' I had to smile. 'He looked on it as weakness. I suspect he couldn't deal with it. Anyhow it always redoubled his fury. He was kind, too, in fits, when he was feeling good about things. That was even more unacceptable. And that phrase from the Bible is true that after enough suffering a kind of iron enters the soul. It's very far from commendable, but now I do want to see it through.'

'Well, then go,' she said. 'I don't understand it but I can see you want to go. Being new, the earliest I can get holidays will be September.'

We had pasta and two bottles of red wine at the flat the evening before I was to leave for the hay, and with talking we were almost late for our usual walk in the Green. We liked to walk there every good evening before turning home for the night.

The bells were fairly clamouring from all corners, rooting vagrants and lovers from the shrubbery, as we passed through the half-closed gates. Two women at the pond's edge were hurriedly feeding the ducks bread from a plastic bag. We crossed the bridge where the Japanese cherry leaned, down among the emp-

ty benches round the paths and flowerbeds within their low railings. The deckchairs had been gathered in, the sprinklers turned
off. There was about the Green always at this hour some of the
melancholy of the beach at the close of holiday. The gate we had
entered was already locked. The attendant was rattling an enormous bunch of keys at the one through which we had to leave.

'You know,' she said. 'I'd like to be married before long. I
hadn't thought it would make much difference to me, but, oddly,
now I want to be married.'

'I hope it's to me,' I said.

'You haven't asked me.'

I could feel her laughter as she held my arm close.

'I'm asking now.'

I made a flourish of removing a non-existent hat. 'Will you
marry me?'

'I will.'

'When?'

'Before the year is out.'

'Would you like to go for a drink to celebrate, then?'

'I always like any excuse to celebrate.' She was biting her lip.
'Where will you take me?'

'The Shelbourne. It's our local. It'll be quiet.'

I thought of the aggressive boot thrown after the bridal car,
the marbles suddenly rattling in the hubcaps of the honeymoon
car, the metal smeared with oil so that the thrown boxes of confetti would stick, the legs of the comic pyjamas hilariously sewn
up. We would avoid all that. We had promised one another the
simplest wedding.

'We live in a lucky time,' she said and raised her glass, her
calm grey intelligent eyes shining. 'We wouldn't have been allowed to do it this way even a decade ago. Will you tell your father that we're to be married?'

'I don't know. Probably not unless it comes up. And you?'

'I better. As it is, Mother will probably be furious that it is not
going to be a big splash.'

'I'm so grateful for these months together. That we were able to drift into marriage without that drowning plunge when you see your whole life in a flash. What will you do while I'm away?'

'I'll pine,' she teased. 'I might even try to decorate the flat out of simple desperation. There's a play at the Abbey that I want to see. There are some good restaurants in the city if I get too depressed. And in the meantime, have a wonderful time with your father and poor Rose in the nineteenth century at the bloody hay.'

'Oh for the Lord's sake,' I said and rose to leave. Outside she was still laughing so provocatively that I drew her towards me.

The next morning on the train home I heard a transistor far down the carriage promise a prolonged spell of good weather. Meadows were being mowed all along the line, and I saw men testing handfuls of hay in the breeze as they waited for the sun to burn the dew off the fallen swards. It was weather people prayed for at this time.

I walked the three miles from the station. Meadows were down all along the road, some already saved, in stacked bales. The scent of cut grass was everywhere. As I drew close to the stone house in its trees I could hardly wait to see if the Big Meadow was down beyond the row of beech trees. When I lived here I'd felt this same excitement as the train rattled across the bridges into the city or when I approached the first sight of the ocean. Now that I lived in a city on the sea the excitement had been gradually transferred home.

Before I reached the gate I could tell by the emptiness beyond the beeches that the Big Meadow had been cut. Rose and my father were in the house. They were waiting in high excitement.

'Everything's ready for you,' Rose said as she shook my hand, and through the window I saw my old clothes outside in the sun draped across the back of a chair.

'As soon as you get a bite you can jump in your old duds,' my father said. 'I knocked the Big Meadow yesterday. All's ready for go.'

Rose had washed my old clothes before hanging them outside to air. When I changed into them they were still warm from the sun, and they had that lovely clean feel that worn clothes after washing have. Within an hour we were working the machines.

The machines had taken much of the uncertainty and slavery from haymaking, but there was still the anxiety of rain. Each cloud that drifted into the blue above us we watched as apprehensively across the sky as if it were an enemy ship, and we seemed as tired at the end of every day as we were before we had the machines, eating late in silence, waking from listless watching of the television only when the weather forecast showed; and afterwards it was an effort to drag feet to our rooms where the bed lit with moonlight showed like heaven, and sleep was as instant as it was dreamless.

And it was into the stupour of such an evening that the gold watch fell. We were slumped in front of the television set. Rose had been working outside in the front garden, came in and put the tea kettle on the ring, and started to take folded sheets from the linen closet. Without warning, the gold watch spilled out onto the floor. She'd pulled it from the closet with one of the sheets. The pale face was upwards in the poor light. I bent to pick it up. The glass had not broken. 'It's lucky it no longer goes,' Rose breathed.

'Well, if it did you'd soon take good care of that.' My father rose angrily from the rocking chair.

'It just pulled out with the sheets,' Rose said. 'I was running into it everywhere round the house. I put it in with the sheets so that it'd be out of the way.'

'I'm sure you had it well planned. Give us this day our daily crash. Tell me this: Would you sleep at night if you didn't manage to smash or break something during the day?' He'd been frightened out of light sleep in the chair. He was intent on avenging his fright.

'Why did the watch stop?' I asked.

I turned the cold gold in my hand. *Elgin* was the one word on the white face. The delicate hands were of blue steel. All through my childhood it had shone.

'Can there be two reasons why it stopped?' His anger veered

toward me now. 'It stopped because it got broke.'

'Why can't it be fixed?' I ignored the anger.

'Poor Taylor in the town doesn't take in watches anymore,' Rose answered. 'And the last time it stopped we sent it to Sligo. Sligo even sent it to Dublin but it was sent back. A part that holds the balance wheel is broke. What they told us is, that they've stopped making parts for those watches. They have to be specially handmade. They said that the quality of the gold wasn't high enough to justify that expense. That it was only gold plated. I don't suppose it'll ever go again. I put it in with the sheets to have it out of the way. I was running into it everywhere.'

'Well, if it wasn't fixed before, you must certainly have fixed it for good and forever this time.' My father would not let go.

His hand trembled on the arm of the rocking chair, the same hand that would draw out the gold watch long ago as the first strokes of the Angelus came to us over the heather and pale wheaten sedge of Gloria Bog: 'Twenty minutes late, no more than usual. . . . One of these years Jimmy Lynch will startle himself and the whole countryside by ringing the Angelus at exactly twelve. . . . Only in Ireland is there right time and wrong time. In other countries there is just time.' We'd stand and stretch our backs, aching from scattering the turf, and wait for him to lift his straw hat.

Waiting with him under the yew, suitcases round our feet, for the bus that took us each year to the sea at Strandhill after the hay was in and the turf home; and to quiet us he'd take the watch out and let it lie in his open palm, where we'd follow the small second hand low down on the face endlessly circling until the bus came into sight at the top of Doherty's Hill. How clearly everything sang now set free by the distance of the years, with what heaviness the actual scenes and days had weighed.

'If the watch isn't going to be fixed, then, I might as well have it.' I was amazed at the calm sound of my own words. The watch had come to him from his father. Through all the long years of

childhood I had assumed that one day he would pass it on to me.
Then all weakness would be gone. I would possess its power.
Once in a generous fit he even promised it to me, but he did not
keep that promise. Unfairly, perhaps, I expected him to give it to
me when I graduated, when I passed into the civil service, when
I won my first promotion, but he did not. I had forgotten about
it until it had spilled out of the folded sheets onto the floor.

I saw a look pass between my father and stepmother before he
said, 'What good would it be to you?'

'No good. Just a keepsake. I'll get you a good new watch in its
place. I often see watches in the duty-free airports.' My work often took me outside the country.

'I don't need a watch,' he said, and pulled himself up from his
chair.

Rose cast me a furtive look, much the same look that had
passed a few moments before between her and my father. 'Maybe your father wants to keep the watch,' it pleaded, but I ignored
it.

'Didn't the watch once belong to your father?' I asked as he
shuffled toward his room, but the only answer he made was to
turn and yawn back before continuing the slow, exaggerated
shuffle toward his room.

When the train pulled into Amiens Street Station, to my delight
I saw her outside the ticket barrier, in the same tweed suit she'd
worn the Saturday morning we met in Grafton Street. I could
tell that she'd been to the hairdresser, but there were specks of
white paint on her hands.

'Did you tell them that we're to be married?' she asked as we
left the station.

'No.'

'Why not?'

'It never came up. And you, did you write home?'

'No. In fact, I drove down last weekend and told them.'

'How did they take it?'

'They seemed glad. You seemed to have made a good impression.' She smiled. 'As I guessed, Mother is quite annoyed that it's not going to be a big do.'

'You won't change our plans because of that.'

'Of course not. She's not much given to change herself, except to changing other people so that they fit in with her ideas.'

'This fell my way at last,' I said and showed her the silent watch. 'I've always wanted it. If we believed in signs it would seem life is falling into our hands at last.'

'And not before our time, I think I can risk adding.'

We were married that October by a Franciscan in their church on the quays, with two vergers as witnesses, and we drank far too much wine at lunch afterwards in a new restaurant that had opened in Lincoln Court; staggering home in the late afternoon, I saw some people in the street smile at my attempt to lift her across the step. We did not even hear the bells closing the Green.

It was dark when we woke, and she said, 'I have something for you,' taking a small, wrapped package from the bedside table.

'You know we promised not to give presents,' I said.

'I know but this is different. Open it. Anyhow, you said you didn't believe in signs.'

It was the gold watch. I held it to my ear. It was running perfectly. The small second hand was circling endlessly low down on the face. The blue hands pointed past midnight.'

'Did it cost much?'

'No. Very little, but that's not your business.'

'I thought the parts had to be specially made.'

'That wasn't true. They probably never even asked.'

'You shouldn't have bothered.'

'Now I'm hoping to see you wear it,' she laughed.

I did not wear it. I left it on the mantel. The gold and white face and delicate blue hands looked very beautiful to me on the white marble. It gave me a curious pleasure mixed with guilt to wind it and watch it run; and the following spring, coming from a conference in Ottawa, I bought an expensive modern watch in the duty-free shop of Montreal Airport. It was guaranteed for five years, and was shockproof, dustproof, waterproof.

'What do you think of it?' I asked her when I returned to Dublin. 'I bought it for my father.'

'Well, it's no beauty, but my mother would certainly approve of it. It's what she'd describe as *serviceable.*'

'It was expensive enough.'

'It looks expensive. You'll bring it when you go down for the hay?'

'It'll probably be my last summer with them at the hay,' I said apologetically. 'Won't you change your mind and come down with me?'

She shook her head. 'He'd probably say I look fifty now.' She was as strong-willed as the schoolteacher mother she disliked, and I did not press. She was with child and looked calm and lovely.

'What'll they do about the hay when they no longer have you to help them?' she said.

'What does anybody do? Do without me. Stop. Get it done by contract. They have plenty of money. It'll just be the end of something that has gone on for a very long time.'

'That it certainly has.'

I came by train at the same time in July as I'd come every summer, the excitement I'd always felt tainted with melancholy that it'd probably be the last summer I would come. I had not even a wish to see it to its natural end anymore. I had come because it seemed less violent to come than to stay away, and I had the good new modern watch to hand over in place of the old gold. The night before, at dinner, we had talked about buying a house with a garden out near the strand in Sandymount. Any melancholy I was feeling lasted only until I came in sight of the house.

All the meadows had been cut and saved, the bales stacked in groups of five or six and roofed with green grass. The Big Meadow beyond the beeches was completely clean, the bales having been taken in. Though I had come intending to make it my last summer at the hay, I now felt a keen outrage that it had been ended without me. Rose and my father were nowhere to be seen.

'What happened?' I asked when I found them at last, weeding the potato ridge one side of the orchard.

'The winter feeding got too much for us,' my father said. 'We decided to let the meadows. Gillespie took them. He cut early—two weeks ago.'

'Why didn't you tell me?'

My father and Rose exchanged looks, and my father spoke as if he was delivering a prepared statement.

'We didn't like to. And anyhow we thought you'd want to come, hay or no hay. It's more normal to come for a rest instead of just to kill yourself at the old hay. And indeed there's plenty else for you to do if you have a mind to do it. I've taken up the garden again myself.'

'Anyhow, I've brought these,' I handed Rose the box of chocolates and bottle of scent, and gave my father the watch.

'What's this for?' He had always disliked receiving presents.

'It's the watch I told you I'd get in place of the old watch.'

'I don't need a watch.'

'I got it anyhow. What do you think of it?'

'It's ugly,' he said, turning it over.

'It was expensive enough.' I named the price. 'And that was duty free.'

'They must have seen you coming, then.'

'No. It's guaranteed for five years. It's dustproof, shockproof, waterproof.'

'The old gold watch—do you still have that?' He changed after silence.

'Of course.'

'Did you ever get it working?'

136

'No,' I lied. 'But it's sort of nice to have.'

'That doesn't make much sense to me.'

'Well, you'll find that the new watch is working well anyway.'

'What use have I for time here anymore?' he said, but I saw him start to wind and examine the new watch, and he was wearing it at breakfast the next morning. He seemed to want it to be seen as he buttered toast and reached across for milk and sugar.

'What did you want to get up so early for?' he said to me. 'You should have lain in and taken a good rest when you had the chance.'

'What will you be doing today?' I asked.

'Not much. A bit of fooling around. I might get spray ready for the potatoes.'

'It'd be an ideal day for hay,' I said, looking out the window on the fields. The morning was as blue and cool as the plums still touched with dew down by the hayshed. There was a white spider webbing over the grass. I took a book and headed towards the shelter of the beeches in the Big Meadow, for, when the sun would eventually beat through, the day would be uncomfortably hot.

It was a poor attempt at reading. Halfway down each page I'd find I had lost every thread and was staring blankly at the words. I thought at first that the trees and green and those few wisps of cloud, hazy and calm in the emerging blue, brought the tension of past exams and summers too close to the book I held in my hand, but then I found myself stirring uncomfortably in my suit—missing my old loose clothes, the smell of diesel in the meadow, the blades of grass shivering as they fell, the long teeth of the raker kicking the hay into rows, all the jangle and bustle and busyness of the meadows.

I heard the clear blows of a hammer on stone. My father was sledging stones that had fallen from the archway where once the workmen's bell had hung. Some of the stones had been part of

137

the arch and were quite beautiful. There seemed no point in breaking them up. I moved closer, taking care to stay hidden in the shade of the beeches.

As the sledge rose, the watch glittered on my father's wrist. I followed it down, saw the shudder that ran through his arms as the metal met the stone. A watch was always removed from the wrist before such violent work. I waited. In this heat he could not keep up such work for long. He brought the sledge down again and again, the watch glittering, the shock shuddering through his arms. When he stopped, before he wiped the sweat away, he put the watch to his ear and listened intently. What I'd guessed was certain now. From the irritable way he threw the sledge aside, it was clear that the watch was still running.

That afternoon I helped him fill the tar barrel with water for spraying the potatoes, though he made it clear he didn't want help. When he put the bag of blue stone into the barrel to steep, he thrust the watch deep into the water before my eyes.

'I'm going back to Dublin tomorrow,' I said.

'I thought you were coming for two weeks. You always stayed two weeks before.'

'There's no need for me now.'

'It's your holidays now. You're as well off here as by the sea. It's as much of a change and far cheaper.'

'I meant to tell you before, and should have but didn't. I am married now.'

'Tell me more news,' he said with an attempt at cool surprise, but I saw by his eyes that he already knew. 'We heard but we didn't like to believe it. It's a bit late in the day for formal engagements, never mind invitations. I suppose we weren't important enough to be invited.'

'There was no one at the wedding but ourselves. We invited no one, neither her people or mine.'

'Well, I suppose it was cheaper that way,' he agreed sarcastically.

'When will you spray?'

'I'll spray tomorrow,' he said, and we left the blue stone to steep in the barrel of water.

With relief, I noticed he was no longer wearing the watch, but the feeling of unease was so great in the house that after dinner I went outside. It was a perfect moonlit night, the empty fields and beech trees and walls in clear yellow outline. The night seemed so full of serenity that it brought the very ache of longing for all of life to reflect its moonlit calm: but I knew too well it neither was nor could be. It was a dream of death.

I went idly toward the orchard, and as I passed the tar barrel I saw a thin fishing line hanging from a part of the low yew branch down into the barrel. I heard the ticking even before the wrist watch came up tied to the end of the line. What shocked me was that I felt neither surprise nor shock.

I felt the bag that we'd left to steep earlier in the water. The blue stone had all melted down. It was a barrel of pure poison, ready for spraying.

I listened to the ticking of the watch on the end of the line in silence before letting it drop back into the barrel. The poison had already eaten into the casing of the watch. The shining rim and back were no longer smooth. It could hardly run much past morning.

The night was so still that the shadows of the beeches did not waver on the moonlit grass, seemed fixed like a leaf in rock. On the white marble the gold watch must now be lying face upwards in this same light, silent or running. The ticking of the watch down in the barrel was so completely muffled by the spray that only by imagination could it be heard. A bird moved in some high branch, but afterward the silence was so deep it began to hurt, and the longing grew for the bird or anything to stir again.

I stood in that moonlit silence as if waiting for some word or truth, but none came, none ever came; and I grew amused at that part of myself that still expected something, standing like a fool out there in all that moonlit silence, when only what *was* increased or diminished as it changed, became only what is, becom-

139

ing again what *was* even faster than the small second hand endlessly circling in the poison.

Suddenly, the lights in the house went out. Rose had gone to join my father in bed. Before going into the house this last night to my room, I drew the watch up again out of the barrel by the line and listened to it tick, now purely amused by the expectation it renewed—that if I continued to listen to the ticking some word or truth might come. And when I finally lowered the watch back down into the poison, I did it so carefully that no ripple or splash disturbed the quiet, and time, hardly surprisingly, was still running; time that did not have to run to any conclusion.

Swallows

The wind blew the stinging rain from the Gut, where earlier in the bright weather of the summer the Sergeant had sat in the tarred boat, anchored by a rope to an old Ford radiator that clung to the weeds outside the rushes, and watched taut line after taut line cut like cheesewire through the water as hooked roach after hooked roach made a last surge towards the freedom of the open lake before landing slapping on the floorboards. The wind blew the rain from the Gut against the black limestone of the Quarry, where on the wet tar, its pools ruffling in the wet wind, the Sergeant and the young State Surveyor measured the scene of the road accident, both with their collars up and hatted against the rain, the black plastic chinstrap a shining strip on the Sergeant's jaw. 'What age was he?' the Surveyor asked, as he noted the last measurement in his official notebook and put the tapewheel in his pocket.

'Eighteen. Wheeling his bicycle up the hill on his way to Carrick, apparently for a haircut, when bang—into the next world via the bonnet, without as much as by your leave.'

'Will you be able to get manslaughter? From the measurements she wouldn't appear to have a leg to stand on.'

'Not a snowball's chance in hell. The family's too well in. You see the wooden cross on the wall there his parents put up, two sticks no more, and they're already complaining: the poor woman has to pass it twice a day on the way to her school and back, and the cross disturbs her, brings back memories, when bygones should be let to be bygones. Her defence is that the sun blinded her as she came round the Quarry. She'll lose her licence for six months and there'll be an order from the bench for the bend to be properly signposted.'

141

The Surveyor whistled as he turned toward his car in the fore-court of the Quarry, his back to the rain sweeping from the mouth of the Gut.

'They're poor, his parents, then?'

'As mountain snipe.'

'Fortunately, Sergeant, you and I don't have to concern our-selves with the justice or injustice. Only with the accurate presentation of the evidence. And I have to thank you for those drawings. They are as near professional as makes no difference. I wish all my jobs could be made as easy.'

'I was good at figures at school,' the Sergeant said awkwardly.

'Why don't you let me drive you back in the rain?'

'There's the bike.'

'That's no problem. I can dump it on the back.'

An evening suit hung in the back of the car, a scarf of white silk draped round the shoulders. On the seat lay an old violin-case.

'You play the fiddle?' the Sergeant noticed, glad to be in out of the rain beating on the windscreen.

'Indeed I do. The violin travels with me everywhere. Do you have much taste for music?'

'When I was young. At the dances. "Rakes of Mallow", "Devil Among the Tailors", jigs and reels.'

'I had to choose once, when I was at University, between surveying and a career in music. I'm afraid I chose security.'

'We all have to eat.'

'Anyhow, I've never regretted it, except in the usual senti-mental moments. In fact, I think if I had to depend on it for my daily bread it might lose half its magic.'

'Is it old, the fiddle? The case looks old.'

'Very old, but I have had it only four years. It has its story. I'm afraid it's a longish story.'

'I'd like to hear it.'

'I was in Avignon in France an evening an old Italian musician was playing between the café tables, and the moment I heard

142

its tone I knew I'd have to have it. I followed him from café to café until he'd finished for the evening, and then invited him to join me over a glass of wine. Over the wine I asked him if he'd sell. First he refused. Then I asked him to name some price he couldn't afford not to take. I'm afraid to tell you the price, it was so high. I tried to haggle but it was no use. The last thing he wanted was to sell, but because of his family he couldn't afford to refuse that price if I was prepared to pay it. With the money he could get proper medical treatment—I couldn't completely follow his French—for his daughter, who was consumptive or something, and he'd do the best he could about the cafés with an ordinary violin. I'm afraid I paid up on the spot, but the experts who have examined it since say it was dead cheap at the price, that it might even be a genuine Stradivarius.'

Streets of Avignon, white walls of the royal popes in the sun, glasses of red wine and the old Italian musician playing between the café tables in the evening, a girl dying of consumption, and the sweeping rain hammering on the windscreen.

'It was in Avignon, wasn't it, if I have the old church history right,' the Sergeant said slowly, 'that those royal popes had their palaces in the schism. Some of them, by all accounts, were capable of a fandango or two besides their Hail Marys.'

'The papal palaces are still there. Avignon is wonderful. You must go there. Some of those wonderful Joe Walsh Specials puts it within all our reaches. The very sound of the name makes me long for summer.'

'I'd love to hear you play on that fiddle.'

'I'm sure that's easily arranged. After all, there's only a few more petty things to check, and then our work is done for the day.'

'We can play in the barracks, then. There's no one there. Biddy can get us something to eat, and then you can play.'

'That doesn't matter at all.'

'Still, the inner man has to be seen to too. Biddy's my housekeeper. She's a good soul, but I must warn you she's deaf as a post and shouts.'

'Let that be the least of our worries,' the young Surveyor smiled indulgently as the car ground to a stop on the barracks' gravel. 'Do you find time hard to kill in this place?' he asked as he got out of the car.

'It's no fun in this weather but in the summer it's fine,' the Sergeant answered while they unroped the bicycle. 'I take out the old boat you see upside-down there under the sycamore. Row it up into the mouth of the Gut and drop the radiator over the side. Time runs like lightning then, feeling the boat sway in the current, a few sandwiches and stout or a little whiskey, and unless there's a bad east wind you're always sure of fish. It's great to feel the first chuck, and see the line cut for the lake.'

'You grill these fish, then?'

'Sometimes Biddy cooks them but mostly I give them away. I don't care about the eating. It's the day in the good weather, and the fishing. I've often noticed that the people mad about fishing hardly ever care about the eating.'

Biddy was turning the handle of the metal sock-machine clamped to the corner of the table when they came into the big kitchen. Its needles clacked. The half-knit sock, weighted with small pieces of lead, hung close to the cement. She didn't turn around. When the Sergeant placed a hand on her shoulder she did not start. She began to shout something to him. Then she saw the Surveyor with the violin-case in his hand at the door, and drew back.

'This is Biddy. She knits socks for half the countryside. More to pass the time than for the few pence it brings her. She's proud as punch of her machine. Pay no attention to her for she'll not hear a word you say.'

The Surveyor changed the violin from his right hand to his left before taking Biddy's hand. 'It's nice to meet you.' As she released his hand she shouted, 'You're very welcome.' The Sergeant went and took a bottle of whiskey and two tumblers from a black press in the corner, its glass covered with a faded curtain, joking uncomfortably, 'I call it the medicine-press,' as the Surveyor opened the violin-case on the table. Biddy stood vacantly by the machine, not sure whether to return to her knitting or not; and as the Sergeant was asking the Surveyor if he would like some water in his whiskey she eventually shouted, 'Would yous be wanting anything to ate now, would yous?' 'Yes. In a minute,' the Sergeant mouthed silently. As soon as he poured the water in the whiskey and placed it beside the Surveyor, who had taken the violin from its case and was lovingly removing its frayed black silk, he apologized, 'I won't be a minute,' and beckoned Biddy to follow him into the scullery. The door was opened on to a small yard, where elder and ash saplings grew out of a crumbling wall. Three hens were perched on the rim of a sawn barrel, gobbling mashed potatoes. As soon as Biddy saw the hens she seized a broom.

'Nobody can take eyes off yous, for one minute.'

She struck with the broom so that one hen in panic flew straight to the window, rocking the shaving mirror.

'Oh Jesus,' the Sergeant seized the broom from Biddy, who stood stock-still in superstitious horror before the rocking shaving mirror; and he then quietly shooed the frightened hen from the window and out the door. He banged the door shut and bolted it with its wooden bolt.

'We'd have had seven years without a day's luck,' she shouted, as she fixed the mirror in the window.

'Never mind the mirror,' he turned her around by the shoulders.

'Never mind the mirror,' she shouted, frightened, to show him that she had read his lips.

'Keep your voice down.'

''Keep your voice down,' she shouted back, and he was desperate.

'We want something to eat.'

'We want something to eat,' she shouted back, but she was calming. 'There's eggs and bacon.'

'Get something decent from the shop. Cheddar and ham, there's salad still in the garden.'

'Cheddar and ham,' she shouted. 'What if his ham is crawling and the price he charges? Not the first time for him to try to pass off crawling ham on me.'

'Go,' the Sergeant said and forced her into a coat he took from the scullery wall.

'Will I pay cash or get it put on the Book?' she shouted.

'The Book,' he handed her a small notebook covered with old policeman's cloth from where it hung from a nail in the wall and rushed her out the door. After he bolted it he whispered, 'Jesus, this night,' and drew his sleeve slowly across his forehead, feeling the braided coarseness of the three silver stripes of his rank, before facing back into the kitchen.

'If you live like pigs you can't expect sweet airs and musics all the time,' the Sergeant said in shame and exasperation as he swallowed his glass of whiskey. The Surveyor hadn't touched his whiskey. He was tuning the strings.

'It'd never do if we were all on the side of the angels,' the Surveyor answered absently.

The Sergeant filled his glass again. He drew up his chair to the fire and threw on a length of ash. The whiskey began to thaw away his unease. He raised his glass to the Surveyor and smiled. He was waiting.

'The Italian street-musician was playing Paganini that first evening in Avignon.'

The bow flowed on the strings, the dark honey of the wood glowing in the early evening: wind gently rustled the leaves of a Genoan olive grove, metallic moonlight shone on their glistening silver as a man and a woman walked in the moonlight in a vague, sweet ecstasy of feeling.

'Wonderful. I've never heard better, not even on the radio,' the Sergeant downed another glass of whiskey as the playing ended.

'Isn't the tone something?'

'It's priceless, that fiddle. You got a bargain.'

'I'm sure the experts are not far out when they say it's most probably a genuine Stradivarius.'

'The experts know. You go to the priest for religion. You go to the doctor for medicine. Who are we to trust if we can't trust the experts? On the broad of our backs we'd be without the experts.'

A man of extraordinary interest was Paganini, the Surveyor started to explain. He was born in Genoa in 1782, of a poor family. But such was his genius and dedication that he brought the world to his feet. In London, the mob used to try to touch him, in the hope that some of his magic might pass over to them, in the way they once tried to touch the hem of Christ's garments—and in the same way they manhandled pop stars in our own day—but nothing could divert him from his calling. Even the last hours given to him in life were spent in marvellous improvisations on his Guarnerius. The Church proved to be the one fly in the ointment. She had doubts as to his orthodoxy, and refused for five years to have him buried in consecrated grounds. In the end, of course, in her usual politic fashion, she relented, and he was laid to rest in a village graveyard on his own land.

'And the church bumming herself up all the time as helping musicians and painters out,' the Sergeant declaimed fervently when the Surveyor finished. 'It'd make a jackass bray backwards. But why don't you drink up? You have more than earned it.'

Apologetically the Surveyor covered his glass with his palm. 'It's the driving, the new laws.'

'Well, I'm the law in these parts, for what it's worth. And there's the C.W.A. party tonight. You could play there. It'd give the ignoramuses there a glimpse past their noses to hear playing the like of the Paganini. You could stay the night here in the barracks, there's tons of room.'

'No. I have to drive to Galway tonight.'

'Well, what's one man's poison. I was never a one for the forcing but that's no reason to stint my own hand,' he said as he filled his own glass again.

'It's your turn now to play, those lovely jigs and reels,' the Surveyor demanded.

'Not since the dances have I played, not for ages.'

'Can't you take the case down anyhow? You never know where the inspiration may come from,' the Surveyor smiled.

The case lay on the long mantel above the fire between a tea-box and a little red lamp that burned before a picture of the Sacred Heart in a crib bordered by fretted shamrocks. Clumsily he got it down: it was thick with dust, his hands left tracks on the case, and the ashes or dust scattered in a cloud when he started to beat it clean with an old towel. The Surveyor coughed in the dust and the Sergeant had to go to the scullery to wash his hands in the iron basin before the mirror. When he came in and finally got the case open, one string of the plain little fiddle was broken. The bow had obviously not been used for years, it was so slack.

'It's no Strad, but it would play after proper repairing. It would be a fine pastime for you on the long nights.'

'Play to old deaf Biddy, is it now. It had a sweet note too in its day though, and I had no need of the old whiskey to hurry the time then, sitting on the planks between the barrels, fiddling away as they danced past while they shouted up to me, "Rise it, Jimmy. More power to your elbow, Jimmy Boy!"'

Going back with the fellows over the fields in the morning as the cold day came up, he remembered; and life was as full of promise as the smile the girl with cloth fuchsia bells in her dark hair threw him as she danced past where he played on the planks. The Surveyor looked from the whiskey bottle to the regret on the sunken face with careless superiority and asked, 'Would you like me to play one of the old tunes?'

'I'd like that very much.'

'Is there anything in particular?'

' "The Kerry Dances." '

'Can you hum the opening part?'

The Sergeant hummed it and confidently the Surveyor took up the playing. 'That's it, that's it,' the Sergeant excitedly beat time with his boots till a loud hammering came on the door.

'Oh my god, it's that woman again,' he pushed his hand through his grey hair, having to go to the scullery door to draw back the bolt.

She was in such a state when she came in that she did not seem to notice the Surveyor playing. 'Wet to the skin I got. And I tauld him his ham was crawling, or if it wasn't crawling it was next door to crawling if I have a nose. Eight-and-six he wanted,' she shouted.

The Surveyor broke off his playing. He watched her shake the rain from her coat and scarf.

'Yous will have to do with bacon and eggs, and that's the end all,' she shouted.

'A simple cup of tea would do me very well,' the Surveyor said.

'But you've had nothing for the inner man,' the Sergeant said as he filled his own glass from the whiskey bottle.

'I'll have to have a proper dinner this evening and I'd rather not eat now.'

'You can't be even tempted to have a drop of this stuff itself?' he offered the bottle.

'No thanks, I'll just finish this. Is there anything else you'd like me to play for you?'

' "Danny Boy", play "Danny Boy", then.'

'Is it bacon and eggs, then?' Biddy shouted.

'Tea and brown bread,' the Sergeant groaned as he framed silently the speech on his lips.

'Tea and brown bread,' she repeated, and he nodded as he gulped the whiskey.

The Surveyor quietly moved into 'Danny Boy', but as the rattle of a kettle entered 'When Summer's in the Meadows', his irritated face above the lovely old violin was plainly fighting to hold its concentration as he played.

'Maybe we might be able to persuade you to stay the night yet after all?' the Sergeant pressed with the fading strength of the whiskey while they drank sobering tea at the table with the knitting-machine clamped to its end. 'It'd be a great charity. Never before would they have heard playing the like of what you can play. It might occupy their minds with something other than pigs and hens and bullocks for once. Biddy could make up the spare room for you in no time, and you could have a good drink without worry of the driving.'

'There's nothing I'd like better than to stay the night and play.'

'That's great. You can stay, then?'

'No, no. It's unfortunately impossible. I have to be at the Seapoint Hotel in Galway at six.'

'You could use the barrack phone to cancel.'

'No. Everytime I get a case in the west I stay at the Seapoint. Eileen O'Neill is manageress there, and she is the best accompanist I know. She could have been a concert pianist. She has already taken the evening off. I'll have a bath when I get to the hotel, and change into the evening suit you saw hanging in the car. We'll have dinner together and afterwards we'll play. We've been studying Kreisler and I can hardly wait to see how some of those lovely melodies play. Some day you must meet her. This evening she'll probably wear the long dress of burgundy velvet with the satin bow in her hair as she plays.'

'I'm sorry I tried to force you. If I'd known I wouldn't have tried to get the C.W.A. function between you and that attraction.'

'Otherwise I'd be delighted. I consider it an honour to be invited. But I suppose,' he said glancing at his watch 'that if I intend to be there by six I better be making the road shorter.' He wrapped the violin in its frayed black silk and carefully returned it to its case. 'What's nice, though, is it's not really goodbye,' he said as they shook hands. 'We'll meet on the court day. And I can't thank you enough for those drawings you made of the accident.'

'They're for nothing, and a safe journey.'

At the door the Surveyor paused, intending to say goodbye to Biddy, but she was so intent on adjusting the needles of the machine to turn the heel of the sock that he decided not to bring his leaving to her notice.

The lighting of the oil-lamp dispelled the increasing blood-red gloom of the globe before the Sacred Heart after he had gone, as dusk deepened into night and Biddy placed suit and white shirt and tie on the chair before the fire of flickering ash.

'Will you be wanting anything to ate before the Function?' she shouted.

'No, Biddy,' he shook his head.

'Well, your clothes will be aired for you there and then when you want to change out of your uniform.'

'Thanks, Biddy,' he said.

'I'll leave your shoes polished by the table. I'll not wait up for you as no doubt it'll be the small hours. I'll put your hot waterjar in the bed.'

'Thanks, thanks, Biddy.'

Quietly he rose and replaced the cheap fiddle in the case, fingering the broken string before adding the slack bow. He shut the case and replaced it between the tea-box and the red globe of the Sacred Heart lamp on the mantel.

The smell of porter and whiskey, blue swirls of cigarette smoke, pounding of boots on the floorboards, as they danced, the sudden yahoos as they swung, and the smile of the girl with the cloth fuchsia bells in her hair as he played, petrified forever in his memory even as his stumblings home over the cold waking fields.

Tonight in Galway, in a long dress of burgundy velvet, satin in her hair, the delicate white hands of Eileen O'Neill would flicker on the white keyboard as the Surveyor played, while Mrs Kilboy would say to him at the C.W.A., 'Something will have to be done about Jackson's thieving ass, Sergeant, it'll take the law to bring him to his senses, nothing less, and those thistles of his will be blowing again over the townland this year with him dead drunk in the pub, and is Biddy's hens laying at all this weather, mine have gone on unholy strike, and I hear you were measuring the road today, you and a young whipper-snapper from Dublin, not even the guards can do anything un-knownst in this place, and everybody's agog as to how the case will go, the poor woman's nerves I hear are in an awful con-dition, having to pass that wooden cross twice a day, and what was the use putting it up if it disturbs her so, it won't bring him back to life, poor Michael, God rest him, going to Carrick for his haircut, the living have remindedness enough of their last ends and testaments without putting up wooden crosses on the highways and byways, and did you ever see such a winter, torrents of rain and expectedness of snow, it'll be a long haul indeed to the summer.'

It would be a long haul to summer and the old tarred boat anchored to the Ford radiator in the mouth of the Gut, the line cutting the water as hooked roach after hooked roach make a last surge towards the freedom of the open lake.

When he had knotted his tie in the mirror his eye fell on the last of the whiskey and he filled the glass to the brim. He shivered as it went down but the melancholy passed from his face. He turned the chair round so that he could sit with his arms on its back, facing Biddy. 'Do you know what I'll say to Mrs Kilboy,' he addressed the unheeding Biddy who was intent on the turning of the heel. 'It'll be a long haul indeed until the summer, Mrs Kilboy,' I'll say. 'And now, Mrs Kilboy, let us talk of higher things. Some of the palaces of the royal popes in Avignon are wonderful, wonderful, Mrs Kilboy, in the sun; and wonderful the cafés and wonderful, Mrs Kilboy, the music. Did you ever hear of a gentleman called Paganini, Mrs Kilboy? A man of extraordinary interest is Paganini. Through his genius he climbed out of the filth of his local Genoa to wealth and fame. So that when he came to London, Mrs Kilboy, the crowds there crowded to touch him as they once trampled on one another to get their hands on Christ; but he stuck to his guns to the very end, improvising marvellously, Mrs Kilboy, during his last hours on his Guarnerius. I wonder what Guarnerius myself and yourself, Mrs Kilboy, or Biddy down in the barracks will be improvising on during our last hours before they hearse us across Cootehall bridge to old Ardcarne? Well, at least we'll be buried in consecrated ground—for I doubt if old Father Glynn will have much doubts as to our orthodoxy—which is more than they did for poor old Paganini, for I was informed today, Mrs Kilboy, that they left him in some field for five years, just like an old dead cow, before they relented and allowed him to be buried in a churchyard on his own land.'

The Sergeant tired of the mockery and rose from the chair, but he finished the dregs of the glass with a flourish, and placed it solidly down on the table. He put on his hat and overcoat, 'We better be making a start, Biddy, if we're ever going to put Mrs Kilboy on the straight and narrow.' But Biddy did not look up. She had turned the heel and would not have to adjust the needles again till she had to start narrowing the sock close to the toe. Her body swayed happily on the chair as she turned and turned the handle, for she knew it would be all plain sailing till she got close to the toe.

Sierra Leone

'I suppose it won't be long now till your friend is here,' the barman said as he held the glass to the light after polishing.

'If it's not too wet,' I said.

'It's a bad evening,' he yawned, the rain drifting across the bandstand and small trees of Fairview Park to stream down the long window.

She showed hardly any signs of rain when she came, lifting the scarf from her black hair. 'You seem to have escaped the wet,' the barman was all smiles as he greeted her.

'I'm afraid I was a bit extravagant and took a taxi,' she said in the rapid speech she used when she was nervous or simulating confusion to create an effect.

'What would you like?'

'Would a hot whiskey be too much trouble?'

'No trouble at all,' the barman smiled and lifted the electric kettle. I moved the table to make room for her in the corner of the varnished partition, beside the small coal fire in the grate. There was the sound of water boiling, and the scent of cloves and lemon. When I rose to go to the counter for the hot drink, the barman motioned that he would bring it over to the fire.

'The spoon is really to keep the glass from cracking,' I nodded toward the steaming glass in front of her on the table. It was a poor attempt to acknowledge the intimacy of the favour. For several months I had been frustrating all his attempts to get to know us, for we had picked Gaffneys because it was out of the way and we had to meet like thieves. Dublin was too small a city to give even our names away.

'This has just come,' I handed her the telegram as soon as the barman had resumed his polishing of the glasses. It was from my father, saying it was urgent I go home at once. She read it without speaking. 'What are you going to do?'

'I don't know. I suppose I'll have to go home.'

'It doesn't say *why*.'

'Of course not. He never gives room.'

'Is it likely to be serious?'

'No, but if I don't go there's the nagging that it may be.'

'What are you going to do then?'

'I suppose go,' I looked at her apprehensively.

'Then that's goodbye to our poor weekend,' she said.

We were the same age and had known each other casually for years. I had first met her with Jerry McCredy, a politician in his early fifties, who had a wife and family in the suburbs, and a reputation as a womanizer round the city; but by my time all the other women had disappeared. The black-haired Geraldine was with him everywhere, and he seemed to have fallen in love at last when old, even to the point of endangering his career. I had thought her young and lovely and wasted, but we didn't meet in any serious way till the night of the Cuban Crisis.

There was a general fever in the city that night, so quiet as to be almost unreal, the streets and faces hushed. I had been wandering from window to window in the area round Grafton Street. On every television set in the windows the Russian ships were still on course for Cuba. There was a growing air that we were walking in the last quiet evening of the world before it was all consumed by fire. 'It looks none too good.' I heard her quick laugh at my side as I stood staring at the ships moving silently across the screen.

'None too good,' I turned. 'Are you scared?'

'Of course I'm scared.'

'Do you know it's the first time we've ever met on our own?' I said. 'Where's Jerry?'

'He's in Cork. At a meeting. One that a loose woman like myself can't appear at,' she laughed her quick provocative laugh.

'Why don't you come for a drink, then?'

'I'd love to. With the way things are I was even thinking of going in for one on my own.'

There was a stillness in the bar such as I had never known. People looked up from their drinks as each fresh news flash came on the set high in the corner, and it was with visible relief that they bent down again to the darkness of their pints.

'It's a real tester for that old chestnut about the Jesuit when he was asked what he'd do if he was playing cards at five minutes to midnight and was suddenly told that the world was to end at midnight,' I said as I took our drinks to a table in one of the far corners of the bar, out of sight of the screen.

'And what would *he* do?'

'He'd continue playing cards, of course, It's to show that all things are equal. It's only love that matters.'

'That's a fine old farce,' she lifted her glass.

'It's strange, how I've always wanted to ask you out, and that it should happen this way. I always thought you very beautiful.'

'Why didn't you tell me?'

'You were with Jerry.'

'You should still have told me. I don't think Jerry ever minded the niceties very much when he was after a woman,' she laughed, and then added softly, 'Actually, I thought you disliked me.'

'Anyhow, we're here this night.'

'I know, but it's somehow hard to believe it.'

It was the stillness that was unreal, the comfortable sitting in chairs with drinks in our hands, the ships leaving a white wake behind them on the screen. We were in the condemned cell waiting for reprieve or execution, except that this time the whole world was the cell. There was nothing we could do. The withering would happen as simply as the turning of a light bulb on or off.

157

Her hair shone dark blue in the light. Her skin had the bloom of ripe fruit. The white teeth glittered when she smiled. We had struggled toward the best years; now they waited for us, and all was to be laid waste as we were about to enter on them. In the freedom of the fear I moved my face close to hers. Our lips met. I put my hand on hers.

'Is Jerry coming back tonight?'

'No.'

'Can I stay with you tonight?'

'If you want that,' her lips touched my face again.

'It's all I could wish for—except, maybe, a better time.'

'Why don't we go, then?' she said softly.

We walked by the Green, closed and hushed within its railings, not talking much. When she said, 'I wonder what they're doing in the Pentagon as we walk these steps by the Green?' it seemed more part of the silence than any speech.

'It's probably just as well we can't know.'

'I hope they do something. It'd be such a waste. All this to go, and us too.'

'We'd be enough.'

There was a bicycle against the wall of the hallway when she turned the key, and it somehow made the stairs and lino-covered hallway more bare.

'It's the man's upstairs,' she nodded towards the bicycle. 'He works on the buses.'

The flat was small and untidy.

'I had always imagined Jerry kept you in more style,' I said idly.

'He doesn't keep me. I pay for this place. He always wanted me to move, but I would never give up my own place,' she said sharply, but she could not be harsh for long, and began to laugh. 'Anyhow he always leaves before morning. He has his breakfast in the other house'; and she switched off the light on the disordered bed and chairs and came into my arms. The night had been so tense and sudden that we had no desire except to lie in one another's arms, and as we kissed a last time before turning to seek our sleep she whispered, 'If you want me during the night, don't be afraid to wake me up.'

The Russian ships had stopped and were lying off Cuba, the radio told us as she made coffee on the small, gas stove beside the sink in the corner of the room the next morning. The danger seemed about to pass. Again the world breathed, and it looked foolish to have believed it had ever been threatened.

Jerry was coming back from Cork that evening, and we agreed as we kissed to let this day go by without meeting, but to meet at five the next day in Gaffneys of Fairview.

The bicycle had gone from the hallway by the time I left. The morning met me as other damp cold Dublin mornings, the world almost restored already to the everyday. The rich uses we dreamed last night when it was threatened that we would put it to if spared were now forgotten, when again it lay all about us in such tedious abundance.

'Did Jerry notice or suspect anything?' I asked over the coal fire in Gaffneys when we met, both of us shy in our first meeting as separate persons after the intimacy of flesh.

'No. All he talked about was the Cuban business. Apparently, they were just as scared. They stayed up drinking all night in the hotel. He just had a terrible hangover.'

That evening we went to my room, and she was, in a calm and quiet way, completely free with her body, offering it as a gift, completely open. With the firelight leaping on the walls of the locked room, I said, 'There is no Cuba now. It is the first time, you and I,' but in my desire was too quick; 'I should have been able to wait,' but she took my face between her hands and drew it down. 'Don't worry. There will come a time soon enough when you won't have that trouble.'

'How did you first meet Jerry?' I asked to cover the silence that came.

'My father was mixed up in politics in a small way, and he was friendly with Jerry; and then my father died while I was at the convent in Eccles Street. Jerry seemed to do most of the arranging at the funeral. And then it seemed natural for him to take me out on those halfdays and Sundays that we were given free.'

'Did you know of his reputation?'

'Everybody did. It made him dangerous and attractive. And one Saturday halfday we went to this flat in an attic off Baggot Street. He must have borrowed it for the occasion for I've never been in it since. I was foolish. I knew so little. I just thought you lay in bed with a man and that was all that happened. I remember it was raining. The flat was right in the roof, and there was the loud drumming of the rain all the time. That's how it began. And it's gone on from there ever since.'

She drew me toward her, in that full openness of desire, but she quickly rose, 'I have to hurry. I have to meet Jerry at nine'; and the pattern of her thieving had been set.

Often when I saw her dress to leave, combing her hair in the big cane armchair, drawing the lipstick across her rich curving lips in the looking glass, I felt that she had come with stolen silver to the room. We had dined with that silver, and now that the meal was ended she was wiping and shining the silver anew, replacing it in the black jewel case to be taken out and used again in Jerry's bed or at his table, doubly soiled; and when I complained she said angrily, 'What about it? He doesn't know.'

'At least you and he aren't fouling up anybody.'

'What about his wife? You seem very moral of a sudden.'

'I'm sorry. I didn't mean it,' I apologized, but already the bloom had gone from the first careless fruits, and we felt the responsibility enter softly, but definitely, as any burden.

'Why can't you stay another hour?'

'I know what'd happen in one of those hours,' she said spiritedly, but the tone was affectionate and dreamy with, perhaps, the desire for children. 'I'd get pregnant as hell in one of those hours.'

'What should we do?'

'Maybe we should tell Jerry,' she said, and it was my turn to be alarmed.

'What would we tell him?'

The days of Jerry's profligacy were over. Not only had he grown jealous but violent. Not long before, hearing that she had been seen in a bar with a man and not being able to find her, he had taken a razor and slashed the dresses in her wardrobe to ribbons.

'We could tell him everything,' she said without conviction. 'That we want to be together.'

'He'd go berserk. You know that.'

'He's often said that the one thing he feels guilty about is having taken my young life. That we should have met when both of us were young.'

'That doesn't mean he'll think me the ideal man for the job,' I said. 'They say the world would be a better place if we looked at ourselves objectively and subjectively at others, but that's never the way the ball bounces.'

'Well, what are we to do?'

'By telling Jerry about us, you're just using one relationship to break up another. I think you should leave Jerry. Tell him that you just want to start up a life of your own.'

'But he'll know that there's someone.'

'That's his problem. You don't have to tell him. We can stay apart for a while. And then take up without any thieving or fear, like two free people.'

'I don't know,' she said as she put on her coat. 'And then, after all that, if I found that you didn't want me, I'd be in a nice fix.'

'There'd be no fear of that. Where are you going tonight?'

'There's a dinner that a younger branch of the Party is giving. It's all right for me to go. They think it rather dashing of Jerry to appear with a young woman.'

'I'm not so sure. Young people don't like to see themselves caricatured either.'

'Anyhow I'm going,' she said.

'Will it be five in Gaffneys tomorrow?'

'At five, then,' I heard as the door opened and softly closed.

'Does Jerry suspect at all,' I asked her again another evening over Gaffneys' small coal fire.

'No. Not at all. Odd that he often was suspicious when nothing at all was going on and now that there is he suspects nothing. Only the other day he was asking about you. He was wondering what had become of you. It seemed so long since we had seen you last.'

Our easy thieving that was hardly loving, anxiety curbed by caution, appetite so luxuriously satisfied that it could poorly give way to the dreaming that draws us close to danger, was wearing itself naturally away when a different relationship was made alarmingly possible. Jerry was suddenly offered a lucrative contract to found a new radio/television network in Sierra Leone, and he was thinking of accepting. Ireland as a small nation with a history of oppression was suddenly becoming useful in the Third World.

'He goes to London the weekend after next for the interview and he'll almost certainly take it.'

'That means the end of his political career here.'

'There's not much further he can get here. It gives him prestige, a different platform, and a lot of cash.'

'How do you fit into this?'

'I don't know.'

'Does he want to take you with him?'

'He'll go out on his own first, but he says that as soon as he's settled there and sees the state of play that he wants me to follow him.'

'What'll you do?'

'I don't know,' she said in a voice that implied that I was now part of these circumstances.

Slane was a lovely old village in the English style close to Dublin. One Sunday we had lunch at the one hotel, more like a village inn than a hotel, plain wooden tables and chairs, the walls and fireplaces simple black and white, iron scrapers on the steps outside the entrance; and she suggested that we go there the weekend Jerry was on interview in London. The country weekend, the walks along the wooded banks of the river, coming back to the hotel with sharp appetites to have one drink in the bar and then to linger over lunch, in the knowledge that we had the whole long curtained afternoon spread before us, was dream enough. But was it to be all that simple? Did we know one another at all, outside these carnal pleasures that we shared, and were we prepared to spend our lives together in the good or nightmare they might bring? And it was growing clearer that she wasn't sure of me and that I wasn't sure. So when the telegram came from the country I was for once almost glad of the usual drama and mysteriousness.

'Then that's goodbye to our poor weekend'; she handed me back the telegram in Gaffneys.

'It's only one weekend,' I protested. 'We'll have as many as we want once Jerry goes.'

'You remember when I wanted to tell Jerry that we were in love you wouldn't have it. You said we didn't know one another well enough, and then when we can have two whole days together you get this telegram. How are we ever going to get to know one another except by being together?'

'Maybe we can still go?'

'No. Not if you are doubtful. I think you should go home.'

'Will you come back with me this evening?'

'No. I have to have dinner with Jerry.'

'When?'

'At eight.'

'We'll have time. We can take a taxi.'

'No, love,' she was quite definite.

'Will you meet me when I come back, then?' I asked uncertainly.

'Jerry comes back from London on Sunday.'

'On Monday, then?'

'All right, on the Monday.' There was no need to say where or when. She even said, 'See you Monday,' to the barman's silent inquiry as we left, and he waved 'Have a nice weekend,' as he gathered in our glasses.

I was returning home: a last look at the telegram before throwing it away—an overnight bag, the ticket, the train—the old wheel turned and turned anew, wearing my life away; but if it wasn't this wheel it would be another.

Rose, my stepmother, seemed glad to see me, smiling hard, speaking rapidly. 'We even thought you might come on the late train last night. We said he might be very well on that train when we heard it pass. We kept the kettle on till after the news, and then we said you'll hardly come now, but even then we didn't go to bed till we were certain you'd not come.'

'Is there something wrong?'

'No. There's nothing wrong.'

'What does he want me for?'

'I suppose he wants to see you. I didn't know there was anything special, but he's been worrying or brooding lately. I'm sure he'll tell you himself. And now you'll be wanting something to eat. He's not been himself lately,' she added conspiratorially. 'If you can, go with him, do your best to humour him.'

We shook hands when he came, but we did not speak, and Rose and myself carried the burden of the conversation during

164

the meal. Suddenly, as we rose at the end of the meal, he said, 'I want you to walk over with me and look at the walnuts.'

'Why the walnuts?'

'He's thinking of selling the walnut trees,' Rose said. 'They've offered a great price. It's for the veneer, but I said you wouldn't want us to sell.'

'A lot you'd know about that,' he said to her in a half-snarl, but she covertly winked at me, and we left it that way.

'Was the telegram about the selling of the walnut trees, then?' I asked as we walked together toward the plantation. 'Sell anything you want as far as I'm concerned.'

'No. I have no intention of selling the walnuts. I threaten to sell them from time to time, just to stir things up. She's fond of those damned walnuts. I just mentioned it as an excuse to get out. We can talk in peace here,' he said, and I waited.

'You know about this Act they're bringing in?' he began ponderously.

'No.'

'They're giving it its first reading, but it's not the law yet.'

'What is this Act?'

'It's an Act that makes sure that the widow gets so much of a man's property as makes no difference after he's dead—whether *he* likes it or not.'

'What's this got to do with us?'

'You can't be that thick. I'll not live forever. After this Act who'll get this place? Now do you get my drift? Rose will. And who'll Rose give it to? Those damned relatives will be swarming all over this place before I'm even cold.'

'How do you know that?' I was asking questions now simply to gain time to think.

'How do I know?' he said with manic grievance. 'Already the place is disappearing fast beneath our feet. Only a few weeks back the tractor was missing. Her damned nephew had it. Without as much as by my leave. They forgot to inform me. And she never goes near them that there's not something missing from the house.'

'That's hardly fair. It's usual to share things round in the country. She always brought more back than she took.'

I remembered the baskets of raspberries and plums she used to bring back from their mountain farms.

'That's right. Don't take my word,' he shouted. 'Soon you'll know.'

'But what's this got to do with the telegram?' I asked, and he quietened.

'I was in to see Callon the solicitor. That's why I sent the telegram. If I transfer the place to you before that Act becomes law, then the Act can't touch us. Do you get me now?'

I did—too well. He would disinherit Rose by signing the place over to me. I would inherit both Rose and the place if he died.

'You won't have it signed over to you, then?'

'No. I won't. Have you said any of this to Rose?'

'Of course I haven't. Do you take me for a fool or something? Are you saying to me for the last time that you won't take it?' And when I wouldn't answer he said with great bitterness, 'I should have known. You don't even have respect for your own blood,' and muttering, walked away toward the cattle gathered between the stone wall and the first of the walnut trees. Once or twice he moved as if he might turn back, but he did not. We did not speak any common language, and to learn another's language is more difficult than to learn any foreign language, especially since its perfect knowledge is sure to end in murder.

We avoided each other that evening, the tension making us prisoners of every small movement, and the next day I tried to slip quietly away.

'Is it going you are?' Rose said sharply when she saw me about to leave.

'That's right, Rose.'

'You shouldn't pass any heed on your father. You should let

it go with him. He won't change his ways now. You're worse than he is, not to let it go with him.'

For a moment I wanted to ask her, 'Do you know that he wanted to leave you at my sweet mercy after his death?' but I knew she would answer, 'What does that matter? You know he gets these ideas. You should let it go with him'; and when I said 'Goodbye, Rose,' she did not answer, and I did not look back.

As the train trundled across the bridges into Dublin and by the grey back of Croke Park, all I could do was stare. The weekend was over like a life. If it had happened differently it would still be over. Differently, we would have had our walks and drinks, made love in the curtained rooms, experimented in the ways of love, pretending we were taming instinct, imagining we were getting more out of it than had been intended, and afterwards. . . . Where were we to go from there, our pleasure now its grinning head. And it would be over and not over. I had gone home instead, a grotesquerie of other home-goings, and it too was over now.

She would have met him at the airport, they would have had dinner, and if their evenings remained the same as when I used to meet them together they would now be having drinks in some bar. As the train came slowly into Amiens Street, I suddenly wanted to find them, to see us all together. They were not in any of the Grafton Street bars, and I was on the point of giving up the impulse—with gratitude that I hadn't been able to fulfil it—when I found them in a hotel lounge by the river. They were sitting at the counter, picking at a bowl of salted peanuts between their drinks. He seemed glad to see me, getting off his stool, 'I was just saying here how long it is since we last saw you,' in his remorseless slow voice, as if my coming might lighten an already heavy-hanging evening. He was so friendly that I could easily have asked him how his interview had gone, amid the profusion of my lies, forgetting that I wasn't supposed to know.

'I've just come from London. We've had dinner at the airport,' he began to tell me all that I already knew.

'And will you take this job?' I asked after he had told me at length about the weekend, without any attempt to select between details, other than to put the whole lot in.

'It's all arranged. It'll be in the papers tomorrow. I leave in three weeks' time,' he said.

'Congratulations,' I proffered uneasily. 'But do you have any regrets about leaving?'

'No. None whatever. I've done my marching stint and speeching stint. Let the young do that now. It's my time to sit back. There comes a time of life when your grapefruit in the morning is important.'

'And will her ladyship go with you?'

'I'll see how the land lies first, and then she'll follow. And by the way,' he began to shake with laughter and gripped my arm so that it hurt, 'don't you think to get up to anything with her while I'm gone.'

'Now that you've put it into my head I might try my hand,' I looked for danger but he was only enjoying his own joke, shaking with laughter as he rose from the barstool. 'I better spend a penny on the strength of that.'

'That—was—mean,' she said without looking up.

'I suppose it was. I couldn't help it.'

'You knew we'd be round. It was mean.'

'Will you see me tomorrow?'

'What do you think?'

'Anyhow, I'll be there.'

'How did your weekend in the country go?' she asked sarcastically.

'It went as usual, nothing but the usual,' I echoed her own sarcasm.

McCredy was still laughing when he came back. 'I've just been thinking that you two should be the young couple, and me the uncle, and if you do decide to get up to something you must ask Uncle's dispensation first,' and he clapped me on the back.

'Well, I better start by asking now,' I said quickly in case my dismay would show, and he let out a bellow of helpless laughter. He must have been drinking, for he put arms round both of us, 'I just love you two young people,' and tears of laughter slipped from his eyes. 'Hi, barman, give us another round before I die.'

I sat inside the partition in Gaffneys the next evening as on all other evenings, the barman as usual polishing glasses, nobody but the two of us in the bar.

'Your friend seems a bit later than usual this evening,' he said.

'I don't think she'll come this evening,' I said, and he looked at me inquiringly. 'She went down the country for the weekend. She was doubtful if she'd get back.'

'I hope there's nothing wrong. . . .'

'No. Her mother is old. You know the way,' I was making for the safety of the roomy clichés.

'That's the sadness. You don't know whether to look after them or your own life.'

Before any pain of her absence could begin to hang about the opening and closing doors as the early evening drinkers bustled in, I got up and left; and yet her absence was certainly less painful than the responsibility of a life together. But what then of love? Love flies out the window, I had heard them say.

'She'll not come now,' I said.

'No. It doesn't seem,' he said as he took my glass with a glance in which suspicion equalled exasperation.

We did not meet till several weeks later. We met in Grafton Street, close to where we had met the first night. A little nervously she agreed to come for a drink with me. She looked quite beautiful, a collar of dark fur pinned to her raincoat.

'Jerry's in Sierra Leone now,' she said when I brought the drinks.

'I know. I read it in the papers.'

'He rang me last night,' she said. 'He was in the house of a friend—a judge. I could hear music in the background. I think they were a bit tight. The judge insisted he speak to me too. He had an Oxford accent. Very posh. But apparently he's as black as the ace of spades,' she laughed. I could see that she treasured the wasteful call more than if it had been a gift of brilliant stones.

She began to tell me about Sierra Leone, its swamps and markets, the avocado and pineapple and cacao and banana trees, its crocodile-infested rivers. Jerry lived in a white-columned house with pillars on a hillside above the sea, and he had been given a chauffeur-driven Mercedes. She laughed when she told me that a native bride had to spend the first nine months of her marriage indoors so that she grew light-skinned.

'Will you be joining Jerry soon?' I asked.

'Soon. He knows enough people high up now to arrange it. They're getting the papers in order.'

'I don't suppose you'll come home with me tonight, then?'

'No,' there wasn't a hint of hesitation in the answer; difficulty and distance were obviously great restorers of the moral order. 'You must let me take you to dinner, then, before you leave. As old friends. No strings attached.' I smoothed. 'That'll be nice,' she said.

Out in Grafton Street we parted as easily as two leaves sent spinning apart by any sudden gust. All things begin in dreams, and it must be wonderful to have your mind full of a whole country like Sierra Leone before you go there and risk discovering that it might be your life.

Nothing seems ever ended except ourselves. On the eve of her departure for Sierra Leone, another telegram came from the country. There was nothing mysterious about it this time. Rose had died.

The overnight bag, the ticket, the train ...

The iron gate under the yew was open and the blinds of the stone house at the end of the gravel were drawn. Her flower garden, inside the wooden gate in the low whitethorn hedge just before the house, had been freshly weeded and the coarse grass had been cut with shears. Who would tend the flowers now? I shook hands with everybody in the still house, including my father, who did not rise from the converted car chair.

I heard them go over and over what happened, as if by going over and over it they would return it to the everyday. 'Rose got up, put on the fire, left the breakfast ready, and went to let out the chickens. She had her hand on the latch coming in, when he heard this thump, and there she was lying, the door half-open.' And they were succeeding. They had to. She had too much of the day.

I went into the room to look on her face. The face was over too. If she had been happy or unhappy it did not show now. Would she have been happier with another? Who knows the person another will find their happiness or unhappiness with? Enough to say that weighed in this scale it makes little difference or all difference.

'Why don't you let it go with him,' I heard her voice. 'You know what he's like.' She had lived rooted in this one place and life, with this one man, like the black sally in the one hedge, as pliant as it is knobbed and gnarled, keeping close to the ground as it invades the darker corners of the meadows.

The coffin was taken in. The house was closed. I saw some of the mourners trample on the flowers as they waited in the front garden for her to be taken out. She was light on our shoulders.

Her people did not return to the house after the funeral. They had relinquished any hopes they had to the land.

171

'We seem to have it all to ourselves,' I said to my father in the empty house. He gave me a venomous look but did not reply for long.

'Yes,' he said. 'Yes. We seem to have it all to ourselves. But where do we go from here?'

Not, anyhow, to Sierra Leone. For a moment I saw the tall colonial building on a hill above the sea, its white pillars, the cool of the veranda in the evening. . . . Maybe they were facing one another across a dinner table at this very moment, a servant removing the dishes.

Where now is Rose?

I see her come on a bicycle, a cane basket on the handlebars. The brakes mustn't be working for she has to jump off and run alongside the bicycle. Her face glows with happiness as she pulls away the newspaper that covers the basket. It is full of dark plums, and eggs wrapped in pieces of newspaper are packed here and there among the plums. Behind her there shivers an enormous breath of pure sky.

'Yes,' my father shouted. 'Where do we go from here?'

'I suppose we might as well try and stay put for a time,' I answered, and when he looked at me sharply I added, for the sake of my own peace, 'that is, until things settle a bit, and we can find our feet again, and think.'

About the Author

John McGahern, born in Dublin in 1934, is a graduate of University College, Dublin. He was the first prose writer to receive the Æ Memorial Award (1962); and in 1964 he was awarded the Arts Council Macaulay Fellowship. He has subsequently received two awards from the British Arts Council and in 1975 the Society of Authors' Travelling Fellowship. His first novel, *The Barracks*, was published in 1962 and his second, *The Dark*, in 1965; a collection of short stories, *Nightlines* (1970), was followed by his third novel, *The Leavetaking*, in 1974, and his fourth, *The Pornographer*, in 1979. His work has been translated into several languages.

McGahern has lived in various parts of the world and his home is now in Ireland.